P9-CFJ-218

THE NINE MILE WALK

Novels by Harry Kemelman:

FRIDAY THE RABBI SLEPT LATE

SATURDAY THE RABBI WENT HUNGRY

THE NINE

THE NICKY WELT STORIES

MILE WALK

OF *Harry Kemelman*

G. P. Putnam's Sons, New York

Third Impression

Library of Congress Catalog Card Number: 67-23130

PRINTED IN THE UNITED STATES OF AMERICA

To Arthur and Doris Fields

Contents

Introduction

Nicky Welt was born in the classroom. I was teaching a class in advanced composition and trying to show my students that words do not exist *in vacuo* but have meanings that can transcend their usual connotations, that even short combinations can permit a wide variety of interpretations. The headline of a story in the newspaper lying on my desk caught my eye—something about a hike planned by the local Boy Scout troop—and I wrote on the blackboard, "A nine mile walk is no joke, especially in the rain." I invited my class to draw what inferences they could from the sentence. As frequently happens with pedagogical brainstorms, the experiment was not too successful. I'm afraid my class regarded it as an elaborate trap and the safest course was to remain silent. But as I coaxed and offered hints and suggestions, I myself was caught up in the game. I made inference upon inference, projection upon projection, and was led further and further. . . .

It occurred to me that I had the material for a story, and when I got home, I tried to write it, but it did not jell. I put the idea aside and a couple of years later, when something recalled it to mind, tried it again. It went no better than the first time. I tried it again several years later, and again several years after that.

Then, fourteen years after my initial try, I tried once again. This time it went. The story flowed, and I knew when I finished at the end of the day that it would require little or no revision. A writer is frequently asked how long it takes to write a story. So there is one answer: it takes one day, or fourteen years, depending on how you look at it.

I sent it off to *Ellery Queen's Mystery Magazine,* where it was accepted almost immediately, along with a letter from the editor promising to buy as many stories of the same type based on the same character as I could write. But it was more than a year before I was able to come up with another.

The Nicky Welt stories attracted attention, I think, because they were the epitome of the armchair type of detective story. The problems were solved by pure logic, and the reader was given the same clues that were available to the detective hero. Furthermore, Nicky Welt was given no advantage, no special powers of intuition, no profound knowledge of criminology. In all candor, this was not so much a matter of choice as of necessity, since I myself had no such knowledge.

Shortly after the publication of "The Nine Mile Walk" I was approached by several publishers who were interested in seeing a full-length manuscript about Nicky Welt. Naturally, I was flattered, but at the same time I felt I had to refuse. I felt that the classic tale of detection was essentially a short story—the primary interest on the problem, with character and setting emerging as adjuncts. Hence to stretch such a story to novel length would call for either engulfing the reader in a tedious recital of every little step that led the hero to his solution—many of these, necessarily, steps in the wrong direction—or posing a problem so complex that the reader would be as puzzled at the end as he was in the beginning. And yet I was intrigued by the idea of writing a full-length book.

The solution was as unexpected—and as logical—as any dreamed up by Nicky Welt.

Some years later, when I moved to the suburbs, I became interested in the sociological situation of the Jew in suburbia. This, I felt, could best be handled in the form of fiction, so I wrote a novel called "The Building of a Temple." I sent the manuscript around to various editors, all of whom wrote me nice notes but regretfully had to decline it.

I had all but given up hope of having it published when fortunately it came to an editor, who, while agreeing that the manuscript as it stood was unsalable, considered the subject itself of enough interest to suggest lines of revision that would make it more suitable for the general public. Moreover, he knew and admired the Nicky Welt stories, which by now had grown into a respectable body of work. . . .

As we discussed the book, once again meanings transcended usual connotations; inference piled upon inference; subjects, characters, events became blended; and what emerged—as in "The Nine Mile Walk"—was a totally new concept, but a solid projection from the original material.

Why not incorporate my detective stories with my novel

of the Jewish suburban community? The traditional function of the rabbi, as opposed to the priest or minister, is as a judge, interpreter of the Law, rather than as a religious leader. How better show this than by getting him involved in a murder mystery and having him work his way out of it?

The solution also had the merit of resolving that problem of the full-length mystery novel. The murder would provide only one thread, albeit an important one, of a larger narrative. That would be the story of the entire community in which the murder occurs and which affects everyone involved. The result, of course, was the creation of the "unorthodox" mystery novels featuring Rabbi David Small—*Friday the Rabbi Slept Late* and *Saturday the Rabbi Went Hungry*.

In a sense, then, Rabbi David Small can be said to be the son of Professor Nicholas Welt.

And now Nicky too is appearing in book form. I am glad, because he has always occupied a special place in my affection. I enjoy reading—and writing—the classic detective story. In fact, the last story in the book, "The Man on the Ladder," is my most recent piece of fiction. Even more, I consider the genre itself important because it is the one modern form primarily dedicated to giving pleasure to the reader. We are apt to forget these days that that is the principal purpose of literature.

H. K.

Marblehead, Massachusetts

The Nine Mile Walk

I HAD made an ass of myself in a speech I had given at the Good Government Association dinner, and Nicky Welt had cornered me at breakfast at the Blue Moon, where we both ate occasionally, for the pleasure of rubbing it in. I had made the mistake of departing from my prepared speech to criticize a statement my predecessor in the office of County Attorney had made to the press. I had drawn a number of inferences from his statement and had thus left myself open to a rebuttal which he had promptly made and which had the effect of making me appear intellectually dishonest. I was new to this political game, having but a few months before left the Law School faculty to become the Reform Party candidate for County Attorney. I said as much in extenuation, but Nicholas Welt, who could never drop his pedagogical manner (he was Snowdon Professor of English Language and Literature), replied in much the same tone that he would dismiss a request from a sophomore for an extension on a term paper, "That's no excuse."

Although he is only two or three years older than I, in his late forties, he always treats me like a schoolmaster hectoring a stupid pupil. And I, perhaps because he looks so much older with his white hair and lined, gnomelike face, suffer it.

"They were perfectly logical inferences," I pleaded.

"My dear boy," he purred, "although human intercourse is well-nigh impossible without inference, most inferences are usually wrong. The percentage of error is particularly high in the legal profession where the intention is not to discover what the speaker wishes to convey, but rather what he wishes to conceal."

I picked up my check and eased out from behind the table.

"I suppose you are referring to cross-examination of witnesses in court. Well, there's always an opposing counsel who will object if the inference is illogical."

"Who said anything about logic?" he retorted. "An inference can be logical and still not be true."

He followed me down the aisle to the cashier's booth. I paid my check and waited impatiently while he searched in an old-fashioned change purse, fishing out coins one by one and placing them on the counter beside his check, only to discover that the total was insufficient. He slid them back into his purse and with a tiny sigh extracted a bill from another compartment of the purse and handed it to the cashier.

"Give me any sentence of ten or twelve words," he said, "and I'll build you a logical chain of inferences that you never dreamed of when you framed the sentence."

Other customers were coming in, and since the space in front of the cashier's booth was small, I decided to wait outside until Nicky completed his transaction with the cashier. I remember being mildly amused at the idea that he probably thought I was still at his elbow and was going right ahead with his discourse.

When he joined me on the sidewalk I said, "A nine mile walk is no joke, especially in the rain."

"No, I shouldn't think it would be," he agreed absently. Then he stopped in his stride and looked at me sharply. "What the devil are you talking about?"

"It's a sentence and it has eleven words," I insisted. And I repeated the sentence, ticking off the words on my fingers.

"What about it?"

"You said that given a sentence of ten or twelve words—"

"Oh, yes." He looked at me suspiciously. "Where did you get it?"

"It just popped into my head. Come on now, build your inferences."

"You're serious about this?" he asked, his little blue eyes glittering with amusement. "You really want me to?"

It was just like him to issue a challenge and then to appear amused when I accepted it. And it made me angry.

"Put up or shut up," I said.

"All right," he said mildly. "No need to be huffy. I'll play. Hm-m, let me see, how did the sentence go? 'A nine mile walk is no joke, especially in the rain.' Not much to go on there."

"It's more than ten words," I rejoined.

"Very well." His voice became crisp as he mentally

squared off to the problem. "First inference: the speaker is aggrieved."

"I'll grant that," I said, "although it hardly seems to be an inference. It's really implicit in the statement."

He nodded impatiently. "Next inference: the rain was unforeseen, otherwise he would have said, 'A nine mile walk in the rain is no joke,' instead of using the 'especially' phrase as an afterthought."

"I'll allow that," I said, "although it's pretty obvious."

"First inferences should be obvious," said Nicky tartly.

I let it go at that. He seemed to be floundering and I didn't want to rub it in.

"Next inference: the speaker is not an athlete or an outdoors man."

"You'll have to explain that one," I said.

"It's the 'especially' phrase again," he said. "The speaker does not say that a nine mile walk in the rain is no joke, but merely the walk—just the distance, mind you—is no joke. Now, nine miles is not such a terribly long distance. You walk more than half that in eighteen holes of golf—and golf is an old man's game," he added slyly. *I* play golf.

"Well, that would be all right under ordinary circumstances," I said, "but there are other possibilities. The speaker might be a soldier in the jungle, in which case nine miles would be a pretty good hike, rain or no rain."

"Yes," and Nicky was sarcastic, "and the speaker might be one-legged. For that matter, the speaker might be a graduate student writing a Ph.D. thesis on humor and starting by listing all the things that are not funny. See here, I'll have to make a couple of assumptions before I continue."

"How do you mean?" I asked, suspiciously.

"Remember, I'm taking this sentence *in vacuo,* as it were. I don't know who said it or what the occasion was. Normally a sentence belongs in the framework of a situation."

"I see. What assumptions do you want to make?"

"For one thing, I want to assume that the intention was not frivolous, that the speaker is referring to a walk that was actually taken, and that the purpose of the walk was not to win a bet or something of that sort."

"That seems reasonable enough," I said.

"And I also want to assume that the locale of the walk is here."

"You mean here in Fairfield?"

"Not necessarily. I mean in this general section of the country."

"Fair enough."

"Then, if you grant those assumptions, you'll have to accept my last inference that the speaker is no athlete or outdoors man."

"Well, all right, go on."

"Then my next inference is that the walk was taken very late at night or very early in the morning—say, between midnight and five or six in the morning."

"How do you figure that one?" I asked.

"Consider the distance, nine miles. We're in a fairly well-populated section. Take any road and you'll find a community of some sort in less than nine miles. Hadley is five miles away, Hadley Falls is seven and a half, Goreton is eleven, but East Goreton is only eight and you strike East Goreton before you come to Goreton. There is local train service along the Goreton road and bus service along the others. All the highways are pretty well traveled. Would anyone have to walk nine miles in a rain unless it were late at night when no buses or trains were running and when the few automobiles that were out would hesitate to pick up a stranger on the highway?"

"He might not have wanted to be seen," I suggested.

Nicky smiled pityingly. "You think he would be less noticeable trudging along the highway than he would be riding in a public conveyance where everyone is usually absorbed in his newspaper?"

"Well, I won't press the point," I said brusquely.

"Then try this one: he was walking toward a town rather than away from one."

I nodded. "It is more likely, I suppose. If he were in a town, he could probably arrange for some sort of transportation. Is that the basis for your inference?"

"Partly that," said Nicky, "but there is also an inference to be drawn from the distance. Remember, it's a *nine* mile walk and nine is one of the exact numbers."

"I'm afraid I don't understand."

That exasperated schoolteacher-look appeared on Nicky's face again. "Suppose you say, 'I took a ten mile walk' or 'a hundred mile drive'; I would assume that you actually walked anywhere from eight to a dozen miles, or that you rode between ninety and a hundred and ten miles. In other words, *ten* and *hundred* are round numbers. You might have walked *exactly* ten miles or just as likely you might have walked *approximately* ten miles. But when you speak of walking *nine* miles, I have a right to assume that you have named an exact figure. Now, we are far more likely to know the distance of the city from a given point than we are to know the distance of a given point from the city. That is, ask anyone in the city how far out Farmer Brown lives, and if he knows him, he will say, 'Three or four miles.' But ask Farmer Brown how far he lives from the city and he will tell you. 'Three and six-tenths miles—measured it on my speedometer many a time.' "

"It's weak, Nicky," I said.

"But in conjunction with your own suggestion that he could have arranged transportation if he had been in a city—"

"Yes, that would do it," I said. "I'll pass it. Any more?"

"I've just begun to hit my stride," he boasted. "My next inference is that he was going to a definite destination and that he had to be there at a particular time. It was not a case of going off to get help because his car broke down or his wife was going to have a baby or somebody was trying to break into his house."

"Oh, come now," I said, "the car breaking down is really the most likely situation. He could have known the exact distance from having checked the mileage just as he was leaving the town."

Nicky shook his head. "Rather than walk nine miles in the rain, he would have curled up on the back seat and gone to sleep, or at least stayed by his car and tried to flag another motorist. Remember, it's nine miles. What would be the least it would take him to hike it?"

"Four hours," I offered.

He nodded. "Certainly no less, considering the rain. We've agreed that it happened very late at night or very early in the morning. Suppose he had his breakdown at one o'clock in the morning. It would be five o'clock before he would arrive. That's daybreak. You begin to see a lot of cars on the road. The buses start just a little later. In fact, the first buses hit Fairfield around five-thirty. Besides, if he were going for help, he would not have to go all the way to town—only as far as the nearest telephone. No, he had a definite appointment, and it was in a town, and it was for some time before five-thirty."

"Then why couldn't he have got there earlier and waited?" I asked. "He could have taken the last bus, arrived around one o'clock, and waited until his appointment. He walks nine miles in the rain instead, and you said he was no athlete."

We had arrived at the Municipal Building where my office is. Normally, any arguments begun at the Blue Moon ended at the entrance to the Municipal Building. But I was interested in Nicky's demonstration and I suggested that he come up for a few minutes.

When we were seated I said, "How about it, Nicky, why couldn't he have arrived early and waited?"

"He could have," Nicky retorted. "But since he did not, we must assume that he was either detained until after the last bus left, or that he had to wait where he was for a signal of some sort, perhaps a telephone call."

"Then according to you, he had an appointment some time between midnight and five-thirty—"

"We can draw it much finer than that. Remember, it takes him four hours to walk the distance. The last bus stops at twelve-thirty A.M. If he doesn't take that, but starts at the same time, he won't arrive at his destination until four-thirty. On the other hand, if he takes the first bus in the morning, he will arrive around five-thirty. That would mean that his appointment was for some time between four-thirty and five-thirty."

"You mean that if his appointment was earlier than four-thirty, he would have taken the last night bus, and if it was later than five-thirty, he would have taken the first morning bus?"

"Precisely. And another thing: if he was waiting for a signal or a phone call, it must have come not much later than one o'clock."

"Yes, I see that," I said. "If his appointment is around five o'clock and it takes him four hours to walk the distance, he'd have to start around one."

He nodded, silent and thoughtful. For some queer reason I could not explain, I did not feel like interrupting his thoughts. On the wall was a large map of the county and I walked over to it and began to study it.

"You're right, Nicky," I remarked over my shoulder, "there's no place as far as nine miles away from Fairfield that doesn't hit another town first. Fairfield is right in the middle of a bunch of smaller towns."

He joined me at the map. "It doesn't have to be Fairfield, you know," he said quietly. "It was probably one of the outlying towns he had to reach. Try Hadley."

"Why Hadley? What would anyone want in Hadley at five o'clock in the morning?"

"The Washington Flyer stops there to take on water about that time," he said quietly.

"That's right, too," I said. "I've heard that train many a night when I couldn't sleep. I'd hear it pulling in and then a minute or two later I'd hear the clock on the Methodist

Church banging out five." I went back to my desk for a timetable. "The Flyer leaves Washington at twelve forty-seven A.M. and gets into Boston at eight A.M."

Nicky was still at the map measuring distances with a pencil.

"Exactly nine miles from Hadley is the Old Sumter Inn," he announced.

"Old Sumter Inn," I echoed. "But that upsets the whole theory. You can arrange for transportation there as easily as you can in a town."

He shook his head. "The cars are kept in an enclosure and you have to get an attendant to check you through the gate. The attendant would remember anyone taking out his car at a strange hour. It's a pretty conservative place. He could have waited in his room until he got a call from Washington about someone on the Flyer—maybe the number of the car and the berth. Then he could just slip out of the hotel and walk to Hadley."

I stared at him, hypnotized.

"It wouldn't be difficult to slip aboard while the train was taking on water, and then if he knew the car number and the berth—"

"Nicky," I said portentously, "as the Reform District Attorney who campaigned on an economy program, I am going to waste the taxpayers' money and call Boston long distance. It's ridiculous, it's insane—but I'm going to do it!"

His little blue eyes glittered and he moistened his lips with the tip of his tongue.

"Go ahead," he said hoarsely.

I replaced the telephone in its cradle.

"Nicky," I said, "this is probably the most remarkable coincidence in the history of criminal investigation: *a man was found murdered in his berth on last night's twelve-forty-seven from Washington!* He'd been dead about three hours, which would make it exactly right for Hadley."

"I thought it was something like that," said Nicky. "But you're wrong about its being a coincidence. It can't be. Where did you get that sentence?"

"It was just a sentence. It simply popped into my head."

"It couldn't have! It's not the sort of sentence that pops into one's head. If you had taught composition as long as I have, you'd know that when you ask someone for a sentence of ten words or so, you get an ordinary statement such as 'I like milk'—with the other words made up by a modifying clause like, 'because it is good for my health.' The sentence you offered related to a *particular situation.*"

"But I tell you I talked to no one this morning. And I was alone with you at the Blue Moon."

"You weren't with me all the time I paid my check," he said sharply. "Did you meet anyone while you were waiting on the sidewalk for me to come out of the Blue Moon?"

I shook my head. "I was outside for less than a minute before you joined me. You see, a couple of men came in while you were digging out your change and one of them bumped me, so I thought I'd wait—"

"Did you ever see them before?"

"Who?"

"The two men who came in," he said, the note of exasperation creeping into his voice again.

"Why, no—they weren't anyone I knew."

"Were they talking?"

"I guess so. Yes, they were. Quite absorbed in their conversation, as a matter of fact—otherwise, they would have noticed me and I would not have been bumped."

"Not many strangers come into the Blue Moon," he remarked.

"Do you think it was they?" I asked eagerly. "I think I'd know them again if I saw them."

Nicky's eyes narrowed. "It's possible. There had to be two—one to trail the victim in Washington and ascertain his berth number, the other to wait here and do the job. The Washington man would be likely to come down here afterwards. If there was theft as well as murder, it would be to divide the spoils. If it was just murder, he would probably have to come down to pay off his confederate."

I reached for the telephone.

"We've been gone less than half an hour," Nicky went on. "They were just coming in and service is slow at the Blue Moon. The one who walked all the way to Hadley must certainly be hungry and the other probably drove all night from Washington."

"Call me immediately if you make an arrest," I said into the phone and hung up.

Neither of us spoke a word while we waited. We paced the floor, avoiding each other almost as though we had done something we were ashamed of.

The telephone rang at last. I picked it up and listened. Then I said, "O. K." and turned to Nicky.

"One of them tried to escape through the kitchen but Winn had someone stationed at the back and they got him."

"That would seem to prove it," said Nicky with a frosty little smile.

I nodded agreement.

He glanced at his watch. "Gracious," he exclaimed, "I wanted to make an early start on my work this morning, and here I've already wasted all this time talking with you."

I let him get to the door. "Oh, Nicky," I called, "what was it you set out to prove?"

"That a chain of inferences could be logical and still not be true," he said.

"Oh."

"What are you laughing at?" he asked snappishly. And then he laughed too.

The Straw Man

IT was my turn to be host to the County Attorneys' Club. It is purely a social organization and calls for little more than a good dinner and an evening of shop talk afterwards, largely pleasant bragging about the interesting cases we had handled since the last meeting.

Fairfield County is a quiet, orderly community where little that is sensational comes our way. Hence, when it came my turn to tell of a clever bit of pleading or of some abstruse legal point which had enabled me to break up a vicious racket, I had nothing that could interest that company and perforce fell back on an account of Nicky Welt's logical reconstruction of a crime and my own meager activities in the case of The Nine Mile Walk.

They heard me out politely, although their attitudes indicated that they thought I was dramatizing the facts a bit in order to improve my story. When I had finished, Ellis Johnston, who as attorney for Suffolk, the most populous county in the commonwealth, was dean of our little company, nodded perfunctorily and said, "That's all very well. Sometimes you get a hunch like that and it works out. But where you have hundreds of cases a year, you can't rely on hunches to solve most of them. You've got to use plain, down-to-earth routine, just plugging away at every little fact you've got until you squeeze out the truth. It's not inspiration but perspiration that solves criminal cases."

The others nodded sycophantically.

"Now here's something that will show you what I mean," he continued. From his inside breast pocket he brought forth a large wallet from which he extracted a square of glossy paper. He tossed it on the table and we all left our seats to look at it. It was a photostat of a ransom note of the type which has become all too familiar these days—little blocks of newsprint pasted onto a blank sheet of paper to spell out the message:

> Fifty Thousand dollars IN ***SMALL USED*** **bills** or GLORIA will **Never** be seen ***again.*** **The Same** IF YOU Communicate WITH **the** POLICE. ***Further Instructions*** **WILL** be **telephoned.**

It was a common enough note, except for one thing: in each block of newsprint, highlighted by the black powder which the police photographer had used, was a clear, unsmudged fingerprint.

Johnston sat back and watched us as we bent over the paper. He was a square, thick-set man with fleshy lips and a determined jaw. And although he owed his position more to politics than to legal ability, he was considered a first-rate man at his job.

"It's routine to test for fingerprints," he remarked, "but we could see these even without dusting. Those squares of paper are not ordinary wood-pulp newsprint. They were cut from glossy-paper magazines like *Life* and *The Saturday Evening Post*, which show fingerprints nicely. Now here's my point. We don't sit down and moon over why a man who goes to such elaborate precautions to conceal his identity should then ruin it all by leaving his fingerprints. In the hundreds of cases that come through our hands we find that criminals are continuously pulling boners like that. In the present case it may be an oversight, or maybe it's just plain swank. We see a lot of that, too. It's almost characteristic of the criminal mind. But whatever it is, we don't let it sidetrack us. We've got a routine, see? And it's routine—with the whole department working together—that solves cases, not inspiration or hunches or the sort of moonbeam inferences your friend the professor used," he added for my benefit.

"We get many cases like this," he went on, "a lot more than the public thinks. The public thinks that kidnappings are rare and that they happen only when they hit the headlines. But actually it's not an uncommon crime at all. Like blackmail, the criminal has every advantage and that tends to make it a pretty common crime. In most cases, the victim pays off within a day or two and that's the end of it. Most of the time they don't even notify the police after it's over—afraid of retaliation of some sort.

"And that's what happened here. Dr. John Regan got that message, paid off two days later, and got his daughter Gloria back. The kidnappers had kept her doped up and so she could tell us nothing. She and her father had gone to the Silver Slipper, a night club and gambling joint. Her father had been called away to answer the telephone. When he got back, the waiter told him that his daughter had met some friends and had gone on to another club with them. There was nothing unusual in that. He stayed on, spent a couple of hours in the gambling rooms upstairs, and then went on home alone. The letter came in the mail the following morning. Later that day, he got a telephone message telling him where to leave the money and where to pick up his daughter. The kidnappers were true to their word, and the following day he got his daughter back."

"And then he called your office, I suppose," I said.

Johnston shook his head. "As a matter of fact, he didn't. This is one of those cases we ordinarily would not have heard of. Even when we did get into it, Dr. Regan was less than cooperative. His point was that he had made a bargain and that he had to live up to it. That's nonsense, of course, but I suppose he didn't like to say that he was afraid. And we couldn't put pressure on him. He's an important man in our town—trustee of a couple of charities, serves on civic committees, that sort of thing. And he's rich. I don't mean the sort of wealth that a fashionable doctor would have. As a matter of fact, he hasn't practiced for years, except maybe on his older brother Philip who had a bad heart and who lived with him. His money comes from real estate. He owns a lot of property in the city. Well, a man like that you can't push around.

"A private detective, name of Simes, who runs the local office for National Investigation, gave us the tip and brought us the note." He gestured toward the photostat on the table. "Philip Regan, the older brother, had called him in. He was not supposed to do any detecting, just to act as go-between and handle the transfer of the money. The idea was, I suppose, that if the doctor himself should try to handle the matter, he might be double-crossed—

pay out money and get nothing in return except maybe a demand for more money. It turned out that it wasn't necessary. The kidnapper called the doctor who followed their instructions and got his daughter back. When I asked him why he hadn't had Simes handle it, he said that he had never intended to and had engaged him only because his brother had been so uneasy.

"Well, the daughter was back and Dr. John Regan wanted to drop the whole matter. But the next day his brother Philip had another heart attack, and died. Simes was bothered by the whole business. There was nothing wrong about the death, mind you. Philip Regan was about sixty and had had a coronary condition for years. He was apt to go at any time. I suppose the excitement of the kidnapping, and the girl coming back all doped up, may have caused it. But Simes was uneasy about concealing the kidnapping, and the death of his client on top of that made him even more uneasy. It was probably just a coincidence, he thought, but on the other hand, there might be some connection. He got in touch with his New York office and they told him to report it to us. The fact that he had dealt with Philip and not with the doctor made it a little easier for him. He was not obligated to follow the doctor's wishes in the matter since, strictly speaking, he wasn't the one who had engaged him.

"Of course, we checked into Philip's death, but there was nothing there that concerned us. He had been suffering from a bad heart for a long time. He did nothing—just hung around the house, puttering in the garden in old clothes, gossiping with passersby over the fence. In the summer he'd sometimes take a few of the neighbors' kids and go fishing. He was a harmless old coot." He brushed aside the idea with an impatient gesture of the hand. Then he smiled a shrewd, self-satisfied smile. "But, naturally, we have to investigate all kidnappings."

He leaned back in his armchair and spread his hands. "There you have the whole picture. Now what are we doing about it? Well, one thing we're *not* doing is trying to fathom why the kidnapper put his prints on the message. As I said, criminals are always making mistakes like that. If they didn't make mistakes of some kind, we could never hope to catch them. We just went right ahead with our routine. We sent copies of those prints down to Washington, on the off chance that they had them on file. They didn't, of course—that was too much to hope for. But we weren't disappointed. You see, when you work on a routine, you know that most of your leads won't amount to anything. It doesn't matter. Sooner or later, one of them does actually lead somewhere, and then you've cracked your case. We had a paper expert go over the message and determine what magazines they had been cut from. You can't tell from the photostat, but just a casual inspection of the original showed that although they were all glossy stock, they came from different magazines. Then we set someone to trying to figure out which issue of each magazine was used. That wasn't too hard because all of those words were snipped from story heads—just tedious routine—and the printing on the reverse of each unit of type helped establish where each came from. When we found out that four different magazines had been used, all current issues, we sent men to call on every bookstore and magazine counter in the postal district from which the letter was mailed. The idea was that some clerk might remember someone coming in and buying a lot of magazines at the same time.

"Then we called in Blackie Venuti, who runs the Silver Slipper, and we grilled him. We wouldn't have been surprised if he had had something to do with it. He's been in some pretty dim activities, and we've had our eye on him for a long time. We didn't get anything out of him, because we haven't got a wedge to open him up with. But he gave us his reservation list, which in turn gave us the names of the people who were at his club that night.

"Of course, that story of Gloria having met some other people and gone off with them is phony. We figure that she may have been called out the way her father was, on the pretext of a telephone message. The waiter said she told him she was leaving and that that was all he told her father. I fancy her father assumed that she had met some people and gone on to another club with them. He was vague about just what the waiter did tell him, when we questioned him a second time. We're planning to question him some more. And we're going to question everyone who was at the club that night. The chances are that she slipped away during the floor show, when the place was pretty dark, but still somebody *may* have noticed her. But"—he held up a forefinger and looked around at us impressively—"one thing we know, and that is that if we can judge by past experience, someone will pop up who saw something or who can give us some sort of clue, and we'll follow that clue until we finally have a case."

He sat back with a self-satisfied air, and I felt that I had been properly squelched. I was going to explain that I had not offered my story as a workable method, when the doorbell rang and I remembered that it was Friday night, my regular evening for chess with Nicky, and that I had forgotten to cancel our appointment.

I hurried to answer the door myself. It was Nicky, of course. He wouldn't forget. He caught sight of the company and looked at me sharply out of his frosty blue eyes. I stammered apologies and then quickly added to mollify him, "We were just talking about you, Nicky. Won't you join us?"

Nicky, Professor Nicholas Welt, Snowdon Professor of English Language and Literature at the university, always treated me like an immature schoolboy, and for the life of me, I always felt like one when I was with him.

He heard me out politely enough, his little blue eyes glittering suspiciously at my company. But he was reserved as he shook hands with each of my guests, in acknowledgment of introductions. When he had made the rounds, Johnston said with a sly look at the rest of us, "Your friend has been telling us of your clever hunch, Professor, which enabled him to break a case. Perhaps you can give us a hand on another problem. What do you make of that little note on the table?"

I expected Nicky to take offense at the suggestion that he acted on hunches, and perhaps he did, for his thin lips were tightly compressed as though he had just bitten into a particularly sour lemon. But he said nothing and moved over to the table.

"That's a photostat," Johnston explained. "The original came to us a couple of days ago. It's not a practical joke. There actually was a kidnapping."

"It came to you with these fingerprints on it?"

"Yes. We dusted them in order to have them show up

in the photostat. It wasn't too hard because those squares of paper are not newspaper but heavy, glossy-magazine stock."

"Indeed? Then that means that those prints are not on there by accident," said Nicky.

Johnston winked at the company and I felt sorry for Nicky.

"You know, Nicky, criminals are apt—" I began, but Johnston shut me up with a gesture of his hand.

"And why could it not have been an accident, Professor?" Johnston purred.

Nicky gave him the annoyed look that he usually reserved for me.

"The average newspaper," he began, in his martyred voice, "has so many more story captions from which a message could be formed than a magazine has that it would seem that the magazine stock was selected *purposely*—obviously, because it does show fingerprints more clearly. These words are all from story headings because the writer wanted big type, but some of them have bits of the regular type showing. Inasmuch as the type faces are different, it would mean of course that several different magazines were used. I suppose that was necessary in order to get all the words needed for the message. It seems hardly likely that the criminal would go to the trouble of checking through several magazines where a single newspaper would have done just as well, if it were not that he wanted this particular type of paper. But there is additional evidence that this was not done in error, or through oversight. I am no expert, but it is plain that there are five different fingerprints here, and they run in a regular sequence. These," he jabbed at the note with a lean forefinger, "are thumbprints, and each one is followed by four prints which represent the remaining fingers of the hand. Even to my untrained eye it appears plain that these prints are of one hand, and that the sequence from thumb to little finger was used over and over again until all the squares of paper had been used up." He looked around at each of us with that amused expression that I have always found so difficult to bear, and then said, "No, no, there is no likelihood of those prints being the result of an accident. They are there for a good reason."

"And what would be the reason for a man to take every precaution to conceal his identity by using printed words and then signing it with the one signature that he could never deny?" asked Johnston.

Nicky cocked a bushy white eyebrow at him. "Surely you can think of a reason," he said.

"Well, it might be intended as a blind to throw us off the track. It could be somebody else's prints," Johnston essayed. And then to bolster his own answer, he added, "It's not hard to lift prints, you know."

"And would it throw you off?" asked Nicky. "All five prints in regular sequence repeated over and over again? If you were able to identify the prints and if you caught the man, would any jury doubt his statement that he had been framed? And how could the writer of the note be certain that the man whose fingerprints he had stolen, as it were, did not have an iron-clad alibi? And even if he did not, wouldn't you be inclined to believe his protestations of innocence, at least to the point of inquiring who his enemies were, and thus be led perhaps to the real culprit?"

Parker of Barnstable County, down the Cape, waved his hand excitedly and Nicky nodded to him.

"Why couldn't the kidnapper have done it for just the reason you said? I mean when he gets caught, he says, 'I didn't do it. Do you think I'd be crazy enough to put my prints on the ransom note?' And so that lets him out, if you see what I mean . . ." Parker's voice trailed off uncertainly.

But Nicky nodded encouragingly at him. "You can see that it wouldn't do," he said gently, "for though you might suspect that the man was innocent, you would be duty-bound to investigate him and to try to make out a case against him. And how could he be sure that you would not find something, once attention was focused on him?"

I tried. "Suppose the kidnapper had something on somebody and was able to force him to leave his prints on the note."

It was only what I expected when he shook his head. "This is kidnapping. Next to murder, it is the worst crime in the calendar. If the man were identified and picked up by the police, he could hardly be expected to take the blame for so serious a crime. But even if he did, it would not end there. He would have to show just how he committed the crime, where he kept the girl, what he did with the money. And of course he couldn't. Besides, if he had been forced to put his prints on the note because of some hold that the real cuprit had on him, would not this in turn give him a hold on his tormenter?"

"Unless he were dead," Johnston interjected.

"Very good," said Nicky. "Force a man to put his prints on the ransom note and then put a bullet through his head and drop his weighted body in the river. An excellent idea, except that the original objection holds. The police would not believe it. If the criminal were planning some such thing, he would have only one print, or better still, only a partial print, appear on the note—so that the possibility of accident might be more readily believed. No, you are quite right in assuming *two* people were involved, but it is a partnership, a voluntary partnership, wherein one partner affixes his prints knowingly and willingly. It would be the logical thing to do if one partner had cause to fear the good faith of the other. For example, if he were afraid that as soon as the enterprise was completed his partner might inform the police, he could make sure of his continued silence in this way."

I'm afraid we all felt a little disappointed. Nicky had taken so high a hand with us that we had come to believe that he really had the answer. This was a complete letdown. Why, there were any number of objections to this theory. Johnston voiced one.

"Why would the partner be crazy enough to do it?"

"Because he is safe," Nicky shot back at him. "He is not a professional criminal. His fingerprints will not be found in any Bureau of Identification."

"Not good enough," said Johnston. "We start hunting and we find something. Just the shadow of a clue. With those prints, that would clinch it. It would be too dangerous."

"Unless, of course, he had every reason to believe that the note would never reach the police," Nicky suggested gently.

"How could he be sure of that?" Johnston demanded truculently.

"By having the letter addressed to his own home," said Nicky.

I don't suppose any of us caught the full implication of Nicky's suggestion.

"Suppose," Nicky went on, "a man with a rich father or brother or a doting aunt needs money badly. He's gambled more than he could afford to lose, or he has been living too high. Or say, he just wants a large sum of money with no strings attached. If he tries to borrow it from his moneyed relative, he will be refused, or he will be expected to pay it back in a certain specified time. But suppose he can go to this same relative and say, 'Dear Aunt Agatha, Gloria has been kidnapped and the kidnappers demand fifty thousand dollars.'? Or suppose the note comes directly to Aunt Agatha who lives with him? Naturally, she would show him the note and in all probability arrange for him to act for her in the matter. Now, how would he go about arranging it? He would seek out some criminal perhaps and outline the plan, and offer him a large portion of the proceeds for sharing in the enterprise with him. Or perhaps the criminal suggests the idea to him in the first place. The criminal—I am not thinking of a petty thief in a sweater and a cap, but a promoter of crimes—what is the slang expression? a big shot—would want to make sure that after it was all over the respectable partner did not hand him over to the police. He would insist that the respectable partner implicate himself unmistakably. The fingerprint method suggests itself immediately."

"Why couldn't he just have the respectable one write out and sign a statement of his participation in the crime?"

"That would be a crazy thing to do," Nicky retorted. "He would be subject to blackmail for the rest of his life."

"Well, isn't he subject to blackmail this way, with his prints on the ransom note?" I asked.

Nicky looked at me in exasperation. "You forget that *he* received the note. He probably sealed the envelope and dropped it in the mailbox himself. It is addressed to himself or to his father or his rich aunt. It arrives at his residence like any other piece of mail. The moment the money is paid off, he destroys it."

"Can't he go to the police then and squeal on his confederate?"

"And how is he going to show that a demand was made for money?" Nicky replied tartly.

We all sat back, each running over in his own mind the composite picture that we could now construct from Johnston's original story and Nicky's deductive analysis of the ransom note.

The more I thought of it, the more convinced I was that Nicky was right. The two brothers living together in a big house. Philip the elder, poor and sick, beholden to his rich successful brother for his very shelter. His strange friends —had it been one of these who had first suggested the plan? Perhaps he did not think he was as sick as his doctor brother insisted. With a large sum of money, Philip could be free and independent. But had Dr. John suspected his brother's implication in the plot against him? Was that the reason Dr. John was now so uncooperative? But why had Philip called in the private detective? That flaw bothered me. Then I saw the whole picture. The doctor, an upright citizen who served on civic committees, had insisted on going to the police in spite of the threat in the note. Philip had been badly worried for a bit, but in the end he had persuaded John to call in a private detective instead. Later the doctor had become suspicious. Perhaps Philip had even confessed just before he died. And now the doctor was afraid to have the police investigate for fear they would uncover his brother's part in the business.

"There's just one little point," Nicky said, seeming to echo my thought aloud. "The partner who received the note was not likely to hand it over to the police. I am curious to know how it came into your hands."

"It doesn't hurt your theory any, our having the note," Johnston said, and proceeded to retell the story as he had originally given it to us. "My guess would be that the criminal partner is Blackie Venuti," he ended.

Nicky nodded. "Yes, I would say that was indicated. Gloria was last seen at his club. Venuti would have no fear of the trail leading back to him, since the whole business, in a sense, was faked. She might even have been held right there in the club all the time."

"We'll sweat it out of Venuti," said Johnston grimly. "Too bad we can't do the same to the respectable partner."

"And why not?" asked Nicky.

"Because as I told you, Philip Regan died yesterday."

"Or was murdered," said Nicky. "It would have been easy enough. The man had a bad heart. A sharp blow to the pit of the stomach would probably do it. If there was a mark, it could readily be explained as resulting from his having fallen against something during his heart attack."

"What do you mean, Professor?"

Nicky shrugged his shoulders. "You see two brothers. Dr. John dresses well and goes to night clubs and serves on civic committees, and all the rest of it. And Philip is sick and lounges around in bathrobe and slippers, unshaven, puttering around the garden. You immediately assume that Dr. John is the rich one, and Philip the poor one." He looked around our little company and his eyes came to rest on Eccles of Norfolk County, a tall, lean, leathery man of sixty-five. Addressing him, he said, "If you had a million dollars, what would you do?"

Eccles smiled. "I'd go fishing nearly every day."

Nicky nodded approvingly. "Precisely. I imagine that's how Philip Regan felt. He had plenty of money and he could do as he liked. So he pampered himself. He dressed when he felt like it, and he didn't shave when he didn't want to. And he could afford to have his younger brother give up his medical practice and dance attendance on him. And John was so addicted to the fleshpots that for the sake of fine clothes and cars and plenty of spending money and social prominence, he was willing to serve as a male nurse to his elder brother. I don't suppose Philip was an easy taskmaster. He was a sick man, for one thing. I fancy he indulged in will-shaking on occasion, threatening to cut off his younger brother without a penny. So Dr. John Regan gambled—in the hope of achieving a certain amount of independence—and lost."

"But we know that John is the one who has the money," Johnston insisted. "He owns scads of real estate in Boston. And it's all his. We looked him up. He is listed in the registry of deeds as owning real estate valued at more than two million dollars."

"No doubt," Nicky conceded. "But I'll wager that somewhere—in the house itself probably, in a good strong safe —Philip had a deed for every piece of property that Dr. John Regan had registry-title to. Our realty law is hopelessly out of date, and for any number of good reasons it is worthwhile to keep one's holdings in a straw name. Dr. John was the straw man in Philip's real-estate transactions. And as you know, Mr. Johnston, the prime requisite of a straw man is that he have no attachable assets of his own. Unless you can get Dr. John to confess, you may never find out exactly what happened, but you can make a pretty good guess. John had lost heavily at Venuti's gambling tables and was deep in debt. Was Venuti pressing him for payment? Did Venuti suggest the scheme?" He shrugged his shoulders. "It makes no great difference. The note was prepared and Philip received it the next day. Since Gloria is John's daughter, and only a niece to Philip, Philip could not go to the police over his brother's objections, but he could insist on bringing in a private detective. Maybe Philip began to suspect something. Maybe he noticed the prints and on his own initiative compared them with those of his brother John—they could readily be found on the furniture around the house. I suppose he made the mistake of telling John that he knew the truth, and intended to notify the police."

"But why couldn't it be the other way round, Nicky?" I demanded. "Why couldn't Philip have been the poor one, the culprit? Why couldn't things be as they appear—that John is the rich one and Philip the poor one? Why couldn't John have wanted to go to the police and been dissuaded by Philip? Why couldn't John's present lack of cooperation with the police be the result of his having learned of his brother's part in the kidnapping?"

Nicky's amused smile brought me to a halt.

"Because," he said, "it was Philip who dealt with the detective and gave him the note. If he had been the culprit, he would never have let the note out of his hands—at least, not without first erasing the prints."

There was silence for a moment. Then Johnston voiced our collective opinion. "It sounds right and tight, Professor, but how can we prove it?"

"You might have some difficulty with the murder," said Nicky. "But the kidnapping plot should be easy. Philip's lawyers would know the real owner of the real estate. The bank would have a record of the account from which the fifty thousand dollars was withdrawn. Dr. John will have to explain *his* fingerprints on the note. Venuti will talk when he realizes that you know the whole story and that he might be tied in with a murder. From here on, ordinary police route should give the necessary legal proof."

He looked around questioningly when we all laughed—even Johnston.

The Ten O'Clock Scholar

I DO not think it was a strong sense of justice that prompted Nicky Welt to come to my assistance on occasion, after I left the Law Faculty to become County Attorney. Rather, I think, it was a certain impatience of mind—like that of the skilled mechanic who chafes as he watches the bungling amateur and at last takes the wrench from his hand with a "Here, let me do it."

Nevertheless, I felt that he enjoyed these brief excursions from the narrow routine of lecturing and grading papers, and when he invited me to attend a doctoral examination, I felt that it was his way of thanking me and reciprocating.

I was busy at the time and loath to accept, but it is hard for me to refuse Nicky. A three-hour doctor's oral can be very dull if you are not yourself the candidate, or at least a member of the examining committee. So I temporized.

"Who is the candidate, Nicky?" I asked. "One of your young men? Anyone I know?"

"A Mr. Bennett—Claude Bennett," he replied. "He has taken some courses with me, but he is not working in my field."

"Anything interesting about his dissertation?" I continued.

Nicky shrugged his shoulders. "Since this is a preliminary examination according to the New Plan, we don't know what the dissertation subject is. In the last half-hour of the examination the candidate will announce it and outline what he hopes to prove. I understand from other members of the committee, however, that Mr. Bennett's interest is primarily in the eighteenth century, and that he is planning to do some work in the Byington Papers."

And now I thought I saw light. I suppose no university is really complete without a faculty feud. Ours was localized to the English Department, and the principals were our two eighteenth century specialists, Professor George Korngold, biographer of Pope, and Professor Emmett Hawthorne, discoverer and editor of the Byington Papers. And so bitter was the conflict between the two men that Professor Hawthorne had been known to walk out of meetings of learned societies when Korngold rose to speak, and Korngold had once declared in a sectional meeting of the Modern Language Association that the Byington Papers were a nineteenth century forgery.

I smiled knowingly. "And Korngold is on the committee?" Professor Hawthorne, I knew, was at the University of Texas for the semester, as an exchange professor.

Nicky's lips twisted into a most unscholarly smirk.

"They're both on the committee, Korngold and Hawthorne."

I looked puzzled. "Is Hawthorne back?"

"We had a wire from him saying that he had made arrangements to return north early, ostensibly to check proof on the new edition of his book. But I consider it most significant that we got the wire shortly after Bennett's examination date was posted in the *Gazette*, and equally significant that he is due to arrive the night before the examination. Of course, we invited him to participate and he wired this acceptance." Nicky rubbed his hands with pleasure.

And although in the nature of things I did not expect to enjoy the proceedings quite as much as Nicky would, I thought it might be interesting.

Like many an anticipated pleasure, however, the actuality proved disappointing. The candidate, Claude Bennett, failed to appear.

The examination was scheduled for ten o'clock Saturday morning, and I arrived in good time—about a quarter of—so as not to miss any part of the fun. The committee had already assembled, however, and I could detect from the general atmosphere, and more particularly from the way the members were grouped as they stood around and gossiped, that Korngold and Hawthorne had already had an exchange or two.

Professor Korngold was a large, stout man, with a fringe of reddish hair. His naturally ruddy complexion was exaggerated by a skin disorder, a form of eczema from which he suffered periodically. He smoked a large curved-stem pipe which was rarely out of his mouth, and when he spoke, the burbling of the pipe was a constant overtone to the deep rumble of his voice.

He came over to me when I entered the room and offering his hand, he bellowed, "Nicky said you were coming. Glad you could make it."

I took his outstretched hand with some reluctance for he was wearing a soiled cotton glove on the other to protect, or perhaps only to conceal, the broken skin where the exzema had penetrated. I withdrew my hand rather quickly, and to cover any awkwardness that might have resulted, I asked, "Has the candidate arrived yet?"

Korngold shook his head. He tugged at his watch chain and brought forth a turnip of a watch. He squinted at the dial and then frowned as he snapped the case shut. "Getting on to ten o'clock," he rumbled. "Bennett better not funk it again."

"Oh, he's been up before, has he?"

"He was scheduled to come up at the beginning of the semester, and a day or two before, he asked for a postponement."

"Does that count against him?"

"It's not supposed to," he said, and then he laughed.

I sauntered over to the other side of the room where Professor Hawthorne was standing. Hawthorne was a small, tidy man, with more than a touch of the dandy about him. He had pointed mustaches, and he was one of the few men in the university who wore a beard, a well-trimmed imperial. He also went in for pince-nez on a broad black ribbon, and even sported a cane, a slim ebony wand with a gold crook. All this since his discovery of the Byington Diary some few years ago, during a summer's study in

England. He had been an ordinary enough figure before that, but the discovery of the Byington Papers had been hailed by enthusiasts as of equal importance to the deciphering of the Pepys Diary, and honors had come to him: a full professorship, an editorial sinecure with a learned publication, and even an honorary degree from a not too impossible Western college. And with it had come the imperial and the cane and the pince-nez on a ribbon.

"George Korngold being amusing at my expense?" he asked with seeming negligence.

"Oh, no," I said quickly. "We were talking about the candidate. George said something about his having funked the examination once before."

"Yes, I suppose Professor Korngold would regard Bennett's request for a postponement as funking it," Hawthorne said ironically, raising his voice so that it was just loud enough to be heard across the room. "I happen to know something about it. And so does Professor Korngold, for that matter. It so happens that Bennett was working on the Byington Papers. Our library acquired the manuscript just a few days before Bennett was scheduled to stand for examination. As a real scholar, naturally he wanted a chance to study the original manuscript. So he asked for a postponement. That's what Korngold calls funking an exam."

From across the room the voice of George Korngold boomed out, "It's ten o'clock, Nicky."

Hawthorne glanced at his watch and squeaked, "It's only five of."

Korngold laughed boisterously, and I realized that he had only been baiting Hawthorne.

When five minutes later the clock in the chapel chimed the hour, Korngold said, "Well, it's ten o'clock now, Nicky. Do we wait till noon?"

Hawthorne waved his stick excitedly. "I protest, Nicky," he cried. "From the general attitude of one member of this committee the candidate has already been prejudged. I think in all fairness that member should disqualify himself. As for the candidate, I am sure he will be along presently. I stopped by at his hotel on my way down and found that he had already gone. I suppose he has dropped in at the library for a last-minute check-up of some point or other. I urge that in all decency we should wait."

"I think we can wait a while, Emmett," said Nicky soothingly.

By a quarter past, however, the candidate had still not arrived, and Hawthorne was in a panic of anxiety. He wandered from one window to another looking out over the campus toward the library. Korngold, on the other hand, was elaborately at ease.

I think we all felt a little sorry for Hawthorne, and yet relieved, somehow, when Nicky finally announced, "It's half-past ten. I think we have waited long enough. I suggest we adjourn."

Hawthorne started to protest, and then thought better of it and remained silent, gnawing on his mustache in vexation. As we all moved to the door, Korngold rumbled loud enough for all to hear, "That young man had better not plan on standing again for examination in this university."

"He may have an adequate excuse," Nicky ventured.

"The way I feel right now," said Korngold, "it would have to be something more than just an adequate excuse.

Only a matter of life and death would justify this cavalier treatment of the examining committee."

Nicky had some work to do at the library, so I went back to my office. I had been there less than an hour when I was informed of the reason for Bennett's seeming negligence. He had been found dead in his room—murdered!

My first reaction, I recall, was the idiotic thought that now Bennett had an excuse that would satisfy even Professor Korngold.

I felt that Nicky ought to be notified, and my secretary tried to reach him several times during the afternoon but without success. When, at four o'clock, Lieutenant Delhanty, our Chief of Homicide, accompanied by Sergeant Carter who had also been working on the case, came to report on his progress, she still had had no luck.

Carter remained outside in the anteroom, in case he should be needed, while I led Delhanty into my office. Delhanty is a systematic man. He brought forth his notebook and placed it carefully on my desk, so that he could refer to it when necessary. Then he carefully drew up a chair and after squinting through his eyeglasses he began to read.

"At ten-forty-five we were notified by James Houston, manager of the Avalon Hotel, that one of his guests, a Claude Bennett, twenty-seven, unmarried, graduate student at the university, had been found dead by the chambermaid, a Mrs. Agnes Underwood. He had obviously been murdered. The call was taken by Sergeant Lomasney who ordered Houston to close and lock the door of the room and to await the arrival of the police.

"The Medical Examiner was notified and came out with us. We arrived at ten-fifty." He looked up from his notes to explain. "The Avalon is that little place on High Street across from the university gymnasium. It's more of a boardinghouse than a hotel, and practically all the guests are permanent, although occasionally they take a transient. There was a car parked in front of the entrance, a Ford coupe, 1957, registration 769214. The key was in the ignition switch." He looked up again. "That turned out to be important," he said. He made a deprecatory gesture with his hand. "It's the sort of thing a policeman would notice—a parked car with the key in the switch. It's practically inviting someone to steal it. It made inquiries of the manager, Houston, and it turned out to be Bennett's car."

"Bennett's room was one flight up, just to the right of the stairs. The shades were drawn when we entered, and Houston explained that they had been found that way. Bennett was lying on the floor, his head bashed in by half a dozen blows from some blunt instrument. The Medical Examiner thought the first one might have done the trick, and the rest were either to make sure or were done out of spite. Near the body was a long dagger, the haft of which was covered with blood. A few strands of hair adhered to the sticky haft and were readily identified as the victim's."

He reached down and drew from the briefcase he had brought with him a long, slim package. He carefully unfolded the waxed-paper wrapper and exposed to view a dagger in a metal sheath. It was about a foot and a half long. The haft, which was stained with dried blood, was about a third of the overall length, about an inch wide and half an inch thick, with all the edges nicely rounded off.

It appeared to be made of bone or ivory, and was engraved with swastikas.

"That was the weapon, I suppose," I said with a smile.

He grinned back at me. "Not much doubt about that," he said. "It fits the wounds just right."

"Any fingerprints?" I asked.

Delhanty shook his head. "None on the weapon, and only the ones you'd expect in the room."

I picked up the dagger gingerly by the sheath.

"Why, it's weighted in the haft," I said.

Delhanty nodded grimly. "It would have to be," he replied, "to have done the job it did on Bennett."

I put it down again. "Well, a dagger like that shouldn't be too hard to trace," I said hopefully.

Delhanty smiled. "We had no trouble with that. It belonged to Bennett."

"The chambermaid identified it?"

"Better than that. The mate to it was right there hanging on the wall. Here, let me show you." Once again he reached into his briefcase and this time came up with a large photograph showing one side of a room. There was a desk against the wall and a typewriter on a small table beside it. But it was the wall above the desk that attracted my attention, for arranged symmetrically on hooks was a veritable arsenal of weapons, each with a little card, presumably of explanation, tacked underneath. By actual count, there were two German sabers, three pistols, two weapons that looked like policemen's night-sticks (at my puzzled look, Delhanty murmured, "Taken from guards of a concentration camp—nasty weapons—almost as thick as my wrist") and one dagger, the twin of the weapon lying on my desk. But there was another card and an empty hook where the other dagger should have been, and it was just possible to discern its outline as a lighter area in the faded wallpaper.

Delhanty chuckled. "G.I. trophies. My boy brought home enough stuff to equip a German regiment."

He drew a pencil from his breast pocket and pointed with it to the desk in the photograph.

"Now I call your attention to this stuff on the desk to the right of this pile of books. It's hard to make out in the picture, but I itemized it."

He referred to his notes again. "Loose change to the sum of twenty-eight cents, a key to the room, a pen and pencil set, a jackknife, a clean handkerchief, and a billfold. It's the usual stuff that a man keeps in his pockets and transfers every time he changes his suit. One thing struck me as funny: the billfold was empty. It had his license and registration and a receipted bill for his room rent and a little book of stamps, but I mean there wasn't a dollar in the money compartment."

"Nothing odd in that," I remarked. "Students are not noted for their wealth."

Delhanty shook his head stubbornly. "Usually you carry some money with you. The change on the desk didn't even amount to lunch money. We searched the place carefully and found no money and no bankbook. But in the wastebasket we did find this."

Once again he ducked down to rummage in his briefcase. This time he brought forth a long government-franked envelope.

"That's the kind they send checks in," he remarked.

"And do you notice the postmark? He must have received it yesterday. So we checked with the local banks and the first one we tried admitted they had cashed a government check for Bennett for one hundred dollars. The teller couldn't be sure, of course, but unless Bennett asked for bills of a particular denomination, he would probably give him the money in three twenties, two tens, three fives and five ones.

"Well," Delhanty went on, "a young man in Bennett's circumstances wouldn't be likely to spend all that in a day. So that suggested to me that robbery might be the motive. And then I thought of the car parked outside with the ignition key still in the switch. It wasn't left there overnight because it would have been tagged. That meant that it was delivered there this morning, either by a friend who had borrowed it, or, more likely, by some garage. We had luck on that too. We found that the car had been left at the High Street Garage for lubrication and was delivered around nine-thirty this morning. When I asked about the key in the switch, the manager of the garage was as puzzled as I had been. They always deliver the keys to the owner, he said, or make arrangments with him to leave them somewhere.

"I asked to look at their records to see who delivered the car. Well, it's only a small place and they didn't keep any such records, but the manager knew that it was a young apprentice mechanic they had there—fellow named Sterling, James Sterling. He does most of the lubricating work and delivers cars when necessary. The manager couldn't be sure, but he thought Sterling had delivered Bennett's car to him several times before. I considered that important because it would show that Sterling knew Bennett's room number and would be able to go right on up without making inquiries."

"I take it," I said, "that there wouldn't be any trouble getting into the hotel without being noticed."

"Oh, as to that, the place is wide open. It's not really a hotel, you see. There's no desk clerk. The outer door is kept open during the day, and anyone could come in and out a dozen times without being seen.

"I asked to speak to Sterling," Delhanty went on, "and learned that he had gone home sick. I got his address and was just leaving, when I noticed a row of steel lockers which I figured were used by the mechanics for their work clothes. I asked the manager to open Sterling's and, after a little fuss, he did. And what do you think I found there, tucked away behind the peak of his greasy work cap? Three twenties, two tens, and three fives. No ones—I suppose he figured he could have those on him without exciting suspicion."

"You went to his home?"

"That's right, sir. He may have been sick before, but he was a lot sicker when he saw me. At first he said he didn't know anything about the money. Then he said he won it shooting crap. And then he said he had found it in Bennett's car, tucked down between the seat and the back cushion. So I told him we had found his fingerprints on the billfold. We hadn't, of course, but sometimes a little lie like that is enough to break them. His answer to that was that he wanted a lawyer. So we locked him up. I thought I'd talk to you before we really put him through the wringer."

"You've done an excellent job, Delhanty," I said. "Quick

work and good, straight thinking. I suppose Sterling thought that leaving the key in the switch would indicate that he hadn't seen Bennett to deliver it to him personally. And you went him one better and figured that his leaving the key in the switch was in itself an indication that something was wrong. Finding the money clinches it, of course. But it would be nice if we found someone who had seen him. You questioned the residents, of course?"

"Naturally, we questioned everybody at the hotel," Delhanty said. He chuckled. "And it just goes to show how sometimes too much investigating can hinder you by leading you off on a tangent. I questioned them before I got a line on Sterling, and for a while I thought I had the logical suspect right there in one of the residents of the hotel. You see we had gone through all the residents, and Houston, the manager, and had drawn a perfect blank: no one had seen anything; no one had heard anything. Then we called in the chambermaid. We had left her for the last because she had been kind of upset and hysterical, what with finding the body and all. Well, she *had* seen something.

"She had started to work on that floor at half-past eight. She's sure of the time because the chapel clock was just chiming. She was just going into the room at the other end of the corridor from Bennett's when she saw Alfred Starr, who occupies the room next to Bennett, leave his room and knock on Bennett's door. She watched, and saw him enter. She waited a minute or two and then went on with her work."

"Why did she watch?" I asked.

"I asked the same question," said Delhanty, "and she

said it was because Starr and Bennett had had a fearful row a couple of days before, and she wondered about his going in now. When I had questioned Starr earlier, he had said nothing about having gone into Bennett's room. So I called him in again and asked him about it. At first he denied it. That's normal. Then when he realized that someone had seen him, he admitted that he had visited Bennett that morning, but insisted that it was only to wish him luck on his exam. Then I mentioned the row he had had a couple of days before. He didn't try to dodge it. He admitted he had had a fight with Bennett, but he claimed he had been a little tight at the time. It appears he had brought his girl down from Boston for a dance at the Medical School a couple of weeks ago. He had been tied up in the morning and had asked Bennett to entertain her. Then he had found out that after she had gone back to Boston, Bennett had written her a couple of times. That was what the fight was about, but he had later realized that he had been foolish. Bennett's coming up for his exam gave him an opportunity to apologize and to wish him luck. He hadn't said anything about it because he didn't want to get mixed up in anything, especially now with final exams on."

Delhanty shrugged his shoulders. "For a while, I thought I had my whole case right there: jealousy over a girl as the motive; weapon and opportunity right at hand; and even some indication of guilt in his not telling a straight story from the beginning. And then the whole case collapsed. The time element was off. The Medical Examiner had figured the murder had taken place about nine o'clock. That didn't bother me too much since the best they can give you is only an approximate time. But Starr was on his way to play squash at the gym, and they have a time-clock arrangement there because there's a fee for the use of the squash courts. Well, according to that clock, Starr was ready to start playing at eight-thirty-three. That would give him only three minutes from the time he entered Bennett's room to the time when he started playing, and it just isn't enough. So there you are. If the time at both ends hadn't been so exact, we would have felt that Starr was the star suspect."

He laughed at his pun, and I managed a smile. Then a thought occurred to me.

"Look here," I said, "there's something wrong with the time even as it stands. I know the arrangement for the squash courts; I've played there often enough. The lockers are at the other end of the building from the courts. You change into your gym clothes first and then you go down to the squash courts and get stamped in. Starr would not have had a chance to change if those times are correct as given."

Delhanty was apologetic. "He didn't change in the gym. I should have mentioned that. The hotel is just across the street, you see. He was wearing shorts and a sweatshirt and had his racket with him when he went into Bennett's room. The chambermaid told us that."

I nodded, a little disappointed. Strictly speaking, criminal investigation is not my job. The police report to me because as County Attorney it is my function to indict, and if a true bill is found, to try the case in court. But it is only natural to seize the opportunity of showing the professional where he might have slipped up.

There was a discreet knock and my secretary opened the door just wide enough to put her head in and say, "Professor Welt is outside."

"Have him come in," I said.

Nicky entered and I introduced him to Delhanty.

"A sad business, Lieutenant," Nicky said, shaking his head. Then he noticed the dagger on the desk. "This the weapon?" he asked.

I nodded.

"Bennett's, I suppose."

"That's right," said Delhanty, his tone showing surprise. "How did you know?"

"I'm only guessing, of course," Nicky replied, with an amused shrug of the shoulders. "But it's fairly obvious. A dagger like that isn't anything that a man would normally carry around with him. And if you went calling on someone with the intent of bludgeoning him to death, it is hardly the sort of thing you would select to take with you. There are a thousand things that are readily available and are so much better for the purpose—a wrench, a hammer, a piece of pipe. But, of course, if you had no intention of killing when you set out, and then found it necessary or expedient, and this was the only thing to hand—"

"But it wasn't," I said. "Show him the photograph, Lieutenant."

Delhanty handed over the photograph with some reluctance, I thought. I got the impression that he was not too pleased with Nicky's characteristic air of amused condescension.

Nicky studied the photograph intently. "These books on the desk here," he said, pointing with a lean forefinger, "are probably the texts he was planning to take to the examination with him. Notice that they all have paper markers. I don't see any notes. Did you find a package of notes anywhere in the room, Lieutenant?"

"Notes?" Delhanty shook his head. "No notes."

"Notes and texts at an examination, Nicky?" I asked.

"Oh, yes, in accordance with the New Plan, you remember, the candidate outlines his dissertation in the last half-hour, indicating what he hopes to prove, listing a partial bibliography and so forth. He is permitted to make use of any texts and notes that he cares to bring with him for that part of the examination."

"Is that so?" said Delhanty politely. "History student, was he? I noticed the top book was History of Cal—Cali—something."

"No, he was an English Literature student, Lieutenant," I said. "But that involves the study of a lot of history. The two fields are interrelated." I remembered that there had been a brief vogue of Moslem influence among eighteenth century writers. "Was it *History of the Caliphate*?" I suggested.

He sampled the title, and then shook his head doubtfully.

I shrugged my shoulders and turned again to Nicky. "Well, why didn't Bennett's assailant select one of the bludgeons instead of the dagger?" I asked. "Excellent weapons for the purpose according to the Lieutenant here—each as thick as his wrist."

"But he didn't use the dagger—at least not to kill with," Nicky replied.

We both stared at him.

"But there is blood on the haft, and some of Bennett's hair. And the Medical Examiner found that it fitted the wounds just right."

Nicky smiled, a peculiarly knowing and annoying smile. "Yes, it would fit, but it is not the weapon." He spread his hands. "Consider, here is a large variety of weapons ready to hand. Would a man select a dagger to bludgeon with when there are actually two bludgeons handy? Besides, hanging there on the wall, how would he know that the haft of the dagger was weighted and could be used as a bludgeon at all?"

"Suppose he planned to stab him, but that Bennett turned before he could draw the blade from the sheath, or say it stuck," Delhanty suggested.

"Then there would be fingerprints showing," Nicky retorted.

"He might have worn gloves," I offered.

"In this weather?" Nicky scoffed. "And attracted no notice? Or are you suggesting that Bennett obligingly waited while the assassin drew them on?"

"He could have wiped the prints off," said Delhanty coldly.

"Off the sheath, yes, but not off the haft. When you draw a dagger, you grip the haft in one hand and the sheath in the other. Now if your victim turns at just that moment and you have to club him with the weighted haft, his prints will be nicely etched in the resultant blood. And you couldn't wipe those off unless you also wiped off the blood or smeared it. That would mean that the murderer would have to have worn at least one glove, and that would be even more noticeable than a pair."

A faint, elusive thought flickered across my mind that

was connected somehow with a man wearing a single glove, but Delhanty was speaking and it escaped me.

"I'll admit, Professor," he was saying, "that I'd expect he would have taken one of the bludgeons—but the fact is, he didn't. We know he used the dagger because it was right there. And it was covered with blood which matches Bennett's and with hair that matches his, and most of all, it fits the wounds."

"Of course," Nicky retorted scornfully. "That's why it was used. It had to fit the wounds in order to conceal the real weapon. The bludgeons wouldn't do because they were too thick. Suppose you had just crushed somebody's skull with a weapon that you felt left a mark which could be traced to you. What would you do? You could continue bashing your victim until you reduced his head to a pulp—in the hope of obliterating the marks; but that would be an extremely bloody business and would take some time. If there was something lying around that would fit the wound nicely, however, you could use it once or twice to get blood and hair on it, and then leave it for the police to find. Having a weapon at hand which apparently fits, they would not think to look for another."

"But there was nothing distinctive about the mark of the weapon," Delhanty objected.

"If you are thinking of something like a branding iron, of course not. But if we assume that the dagger haft was selected because it fitted the original wound, it automatically gives us the shape of the real weapon. Since it was the edge of the haft that was used, I should surmise that the real weapon was smooth and rounded, or round, and about half an inch in diameter. It would have to be something that the attacker could have with him without exciting comment."

"A squash racket!" I cried.

Nicky turned sharply. "What are you talking about?" he asked.

I told him about Starr. "He was dressed in his gym clothes and he had his squash racket with him. The frame of a squash racket would about fit those dimensions. And it would excite no comment from Bennett since Starr was in shorts and sweatshirt."

Nicky pursed his lips and considered. "Is there any reason for supposing that the mark of a squash racket would implicate him?" he asked.

"He was seen by the chambermaid to go into the room."

"That's true enough," Nicky conceded, "although I gathered from your story that he did not know he had been seen."

Before I could answer, Delhanty spoke up. "Of course," he said sarcastically, "I'm nothing but a cop, and all these theories are a little over my head. But I've made an arrest and it was done through ordinary police work on the basis of evidence. Maybe I shouldn't have wasted my time, and my men's time, with legwork and just sat back and dreamed the answer. But there's pretty good proof that Bennett was robbed of a hundred dollars this morning, and I've got a man in a cell right now who had that hundred dollars on him and who hasn't been able to give any explanation that would satisfy a child as to how it got there." He sat back with an air of having put Nicky, and me too, I suspect, in our places.

"Indeed! And how did you go about finding this individual?"

Delhanty shrugged his shoulders in a superior sort of way and did not answer. So I explained about the envelope and billfold clues, and how they had been tracked down.

Nicky listened attentively and then said quietly, "The mechanic arrived around nine-thirty. Have you considered the possibility, Lieutenant, that Bennett was already dead at the time, and that Sterling's crime was not of having killed, but only of having robbed? Much more likely, I assure you. The man would be an idiot to kill, especially for so small a sum, when he knows that he would be suspected almost immediately—after all, his employer knew where he was going and the approximate time that he would arrive. But if he found the man already dead and he saw the money in the wallet, it would be fairly safe to take it. Even if the police were to discover that a sum of money was missing, which was unlikely in the first place, they would normally assume that it had been taken by the murderer. So he probably took the money and then went back to the shop prepared to say, if he should be asked, that he had knocked on Bennett's door to deliver the keys and Bennett had not answered."

"That sounds reasonable, Nicky," I said. Then noticing the look on Delhanty's face, I quickly added, "But it's only a theory. And we know that criminals are guilty of idiotic acts as well as criminal ones. Now if we knew exactly when Bennett was killed, we'd know whether Sterling could be completely eliminated, or if he was still a suspect."

"You could always get the Medical Examiner to swear that it couldn't have happened after nine," Delhanty murmured sarcastically.

I ignored the remark. Besides, it occurred to me that we had overlooked a possible bit of evidence.

"Look, Nicky," I said, "do you remember Emmett Hawthorne saying that he called on Bennett on his way down to the exam? Bennett must already have been dead, which is why he didn't answer and why Emmett concluded that he had gone on ahead. Maybe Emmett remembers what time it was. If it was before nine-thirty, it would at least clear Sterling."

Nicky gave me a nod of approval, and I felt inordinately pleased with myself. It happened so seldom.

I reached for the telephone. "Do you know where he's staying, Nicky? I'll ring him."

"He's staying at the Ambassador," Nicky answered, "but I doubt if he's there now. He was in his cubicle in the library stacks when I left, and there's no phone connection except at the center desk of the Reading Room. If you had a messenger, you might send him over and ask him to come here. I don't think he'd mind. I'm sure he'd be interested in our discussion."

"Sergeant Carter is outside chinning with your secretary," said Delhanty grudgingly. "I could have him go. Where is it?"

"It's a regular rabbit warren of a place," I said. I looked at Nicky. "Perhaps you could go out and give him directions—"

"Perhaps I'd better," said Nicky, and crossed the room to the door.

I smiled inwardly while we waited for him to return. I did not see how Starr's alibi could be broken, but I was sure that Nicky did. When he returned a minute or two later, however, his first words were discouraging.

"Your idea of Starr and the squash racket," he said, "is not entirely devoid of ingenuity, but it won't do. Consider: the original quarrel was about a girl and it occurred a couple of days ago. Now if the two young men are living in the same house—on the same floor, in fact—and Bennett was probably around most of the time, since he was preparing for his exam, why didn't Starr seek him out earlier? It is most unlikely that he would have brooded over the matter for two whole days, and then bright and early on the morning of the third day, on his way to play squash, have stopped off and killed him. Absurd! It would not be beyond the bounds of possibility if Starr had dropped in to warn him off or to threaten him, and then in the course of the quarrel that might have followed, killed him. But in that event there would have been voices raised in anger, and the noise would have been heard by the chambermaid, who was listening for it. There would have been some sign of a struggle—and there was none."

He shook his head. "No, no, I'm afraid you don't grasp the full significance of the dagger and the necessity for its use.

"Look at it this way," he continued. "Suppose the attacker had not used the dagger as a red herring. Suppose that after having bludgeoned Bennett with the weapon he had brought with him, he had departed. What line of investigation would the police have pursued then? On the basis of the wound, the Medical Examiner would describe the weapon as a blunt instrument, round or rounded, and about half an inch in diameter. A length of narrow pipe, or a heavy steel rod would fit, but the assailant couldn't walk around or come into Bennett's room carrying something like that without exciting comment and suspicion. Of course, he could carry it concealed—up his coat sleeve, perhaps. It would be awkward, but it could be managed.

And it would be still more awkward to draw out without Bennett seeing and making an outcry. But again, with luck it could be managed. All this if the attacker set out with the deliberate idea of murdering. But sooner or later, the police would consider the possibility of the crime having been committed on the spur of the moment. And then it would occur to them that the weapon would have to be something that the attacker had with him, something he could carry openly without exciting the slightest suspicion. And that could only be—"

"*A cane!*" I exclaimed.

"Precisely," said Nicky. "And when you think of a cane, Professor Hawthorne is the first person who comes to mind."

"Are you serious, Nicky?"

"Why not? It's an important part of the rather theatrical costume he designed to go with the new personality he acquired since becoming a great man. You can readily see that in his mind, at least, the mark of his cane would identify him as surely as if he had branded the young man with his initials."

"But why would he want to kill his protégé?"

"Because he wasn't—wasn't his protégé, I mean. You remember the young man was scheduled to come up for examination at the beginning of the semester and did not. Hawthorne told us that it was because our library had acquired the original Byington Papers and that Bennett wanted a chance to study them. But the Byington Papers had been published in full, and it is only a short summary of this dissertation that the candidate expounds at the exam. So that even if the original manuscript were to furnish additional proof of his thesis, it would not justify postponing the exam. Hence, we must conclude that Bennett had got an idea for an entirely new dissertation. Naturally, he told Hawthorne about it. But Hawthorne had to go down to Texas, so he probably got Bennett to say nothing of his discovery until his return. Then when announcement was made of the new edition of Hawthorne's book, Bennett decided to stand for examination again. Hawthorne came back as soon as he found out. He arrived last night and this morning was his first chance to see Bennett. I am quite sure he did not come intending to kill him. He would have brought another weapon if he had. He came to beg him to hold off again until they could work out something together—a paper on which they would collaborate, perhaps. I don't think it occurred to Hawthorne that Bennett might refuse. But he did, probably because he felt that after the announcement of a new edition of the Byington Papers he could no longer trust Hawthorne.

"To Hawthorne, this refusal meant the loss of everything he held dear—his academic standing, his reputation as a scholar, his position in the university. So he raised his cane and struck."

"But what discovery could Bennett have made that would justify Hawthorne's killing him?" I asked.

Nicky's eyebrows rose. "I should think you could guess that. We know that Bennett's dissertation subject had something to do with the original manuscript. My guess would be that the book that you noticed on his desk, Lieutenant, was *A History of Calligraphy*—two 'l's,' Lieutenant—a history of handwriting." (The look of sudden recognition that lit up Delhanty's face confirmed the guess.) "I fancy the other books were probably concerned with paper and the chemistry of ink—that sort of thing. In any case, I am quite certain that Bennett had discovered some proof—scientific proof, not internal criticism like Korngold's which is always subject to different interpretations—but proof of handwriting styles and ink and paper that the Byington Papers were a forgery."

The telephone exploded into sound and when I lifted the instrument to my ear, I heard the excited, panicky voice of Sergeant Carter.

"He just shot himself," he cried. "Professor Hawthorne just shot himself here at the hotel!"

I glanced at the two men in the room and saw that they had heard. Delhanty had risen and was reaching for his hat.

"Stay there," I said into the phone. "Lieutenant Delhanty will be there in a minute. What happened?"

"I don't know," Carter answered. "I went to the library but he had just gone. I caught him at the hotel here and I gave him Professor Welt's message. He just nodded and went into the next room, and a couple of seconds later there was a shot."

"All right, stand by." I cradled the phone.

Delhanty was already at the door. "That's it," I said to him.

"Guess so," he muttered, and closed the door behind him.

I turned to Nicky. "What message did you ask Carter to give him?"

He smiled. "Oh, that? I merely suggested to the Sergeant that he ask Hawthorne to bring Bennett's notes with him."

I nodded moodily. For a minute or two I was silent, staring at the desk in front of me. Then I looked up.

"Look here, Nicky, did you expect that your request would have the effect it did?"

He pursed his lips as if to take thought. Then he shrugged his shoulders. "I did not consider it beyond the bounds of possibility. However, my primary concern was my responsibility to poor Bennett. I thought that if there was any merit in his idea, I ought to expand his notes into a paper which I would publish in his name." His little blue eyes glittered and his lips relaxed in a frosty smile. "Naturally, I wanted to begin as soon as possible."

End Play

IT was Friday, my regular evening for chess with Nicky, a custom begun when I had first joined the Law Faculty at the university and continued even after I had given up teaching to become County Attorney. I had just announced a mate in three more moves to win the rubber game of our usual three game match.

Nicky's bushy white eyebrows came together as he scrutinized the corner of the board where my attack was focused. Then he nodded briskly in admission of defeat.

"You might have prevented it," I offered, "if you had advanced the pawn."

"I suppose so," he replied, his little blue eyes glittering with amusement, "but it would only have prolonged the game and the position was beginning to bore me."

I was on the point of retorting that he was most apt to be bored by the position when he was losing, when the doorbell rang and I rose to answer it. It seemed as if I was always being interrupted whenever I had a chance to answer Nicky in kind.

My caller proved to be Colonel Edwards of Army Intelligence who was collaborating with me on the investigation of the death of Professor McNulty. Perhaps it would be fairer to say that we were both investigating the same case rather than that we were collaborating, for there had been an ill-concealed rivalry in our association from the beginning, and we had both gone our separate ways, each working on that phase of the problem that seemed to him most likely to bear fruit. True, we had agreed to meet in my office every morning and discuss our progress, but there was no doubt that each of us was as much concerned with being the first to solve the case as to bring it to a successful conclusion. Since I had had a conference with Colonel Edwards that morning and expected to have another the following morning, his appearance now gave me a vague feeling of uneasiness.

He was a young man, little more than thirty, entirely too young in my opinion to sport eagles. He was short and stocky with something like a strut in his walk, not uncommon in men of that build, and not necessarily indicating conceit. He was a decent chap, I suppose, and probably good at his job, but I did not warm to him and had not from the beginning of our association some two days before. In part, this was due to his insistence, when we had first met, that he should have full charge of the investigation inasmuch as Professor McNulty had been engaged in research for the Army; in part, it was due to his insufferable arrogance. Although he was half a head shorter than I, he somehow contrived to look down his pudgy nose at me.

"I saw a light in your study as I was passing," he explained.

I nodded.

"I thought I'd like to go over certain points with you and get the benefit of your experience," he continued.

That was his usual style and it annoyed me because I was never quite sure whether this seeming deference was his idea of politeness or whether it was downright impudence, said with tongue in cheek. In any case, I did not take it at face value.

I nodded again and led him into the study where Nicky was putting the chessmen back in the box. After I had introduced the two men and we were all seated again, Edwards asked, "Have you uncovered anything important since this morning?"

It flitted across my mind that it was customary for the visiting team to go to bat first, but to have said so would have been to bring our antagonism out into the open.

"Well, we caught Trowbridge," I said. "We found him in Boston and brought him back."

"That was quick work," he said patronizingly, "but I'm afraid you're barking up the wrong tree."

I should have answered that with a shrug of the shoulders, but I felt that I had a strong case, so I said quietly, "He quarreled with McNulty some few hours before he was shot. McNulty had flunked him in his physics course because he had not had his experiments for the semester done in time. He came to see him to explain that he had been handicapped because he had sprained his wrist and so had been unable to write. McNulty was upset and out of sorts that day. Never a very amiable man, he was downright nasty during the interview. I got that from his secretary who was sitting right outside the door of his office and heard most of it. She reported that McNulty had said point-blank that he thought Trowbridge was exaggerating his injury, and even suggested that the young man had managed to get a medical discharge from the Army by the same trick. Parenthetically, I might say, I checked the young man's Army record and found it excellent. He did not get his discharge until after he had been wounded in action twice. Naturally, Trowbridge did not take McNulty's sneer in silence. There was quite a row and the young man was heard by the secretary to say, 'You deserve to be shot.' " I paused impressively.

"Very well," I went on, "we know that Trowbridge took the eight-ten train to Boston. He had to pass McNulty's house on his way to the station and that was no later than eight-five. According to Professor Albrecht, McNulty was shot at a minute or two after eight." I paused again to give added weight to the highly suggestive significance of the time elements. Then I said in quiet triumph, "Under the circumstances, I would say that Trowbridge was a logical suspect." I counted off the points on my fingers. "He quarreled with him and threatened him—that's motive; he had been in the Army and had fought overseas and so was likely to have a German Luger as a war trophy—that's weapon; he was near the house at the time—that's opportunity; and finally, he ran off to Boston—that's indication of guilt."

"But you don't shoot a professor because he flunks you in a course," Edwards objected.

"No, you don't ordinarily," I admitted. "But values change. Trowbridge had fought overseas. I fancy he saw a lot of killing and came to have a much lower opinion of the sanctity of human life. Besides, flunking this course meant dropping out of college. He claims, as a matter of fact, that he came up to Boston to see about the chances of transferring to one of the colleges there. A nervous sensitive young man could easily convince himself that his whole future had been ruined."

Edwards nodded slowly as if to grant me the point. "You questioned him?" he asked.

"I did. I didn't get a confession, if that's what you're thinking. But I did get something. Knowing that he must have passed McNulty's house around eight-five, I told him that he had been seen there. It was just a shot in the dark, of course, and yet not too improbable. The Albany train pulls in around then and there are always two or three passengers who get off here. Going toward town, they'd be likely to pass him on his way to the station."

Edwards nodded again.

"It worked," I went on. "He got very red and finally admitted that he had stopped opposite McNulty's house. He said that he stood there for a few minutes debating whether to see him again and try to get him to change his mind. And then he heard the Albany train pulling in and knowing that the Boston train left soon after, he hurried off. I'm holding him as a material witness. I'll question him again tomorrow after he has spent a night in jail. Maybe I'll get some more out of him then."

Colonel Edwards shook his head slowly. "I doubt if you'll get any more out of him," he said. "Trowbridge didn't shoot him. McNulty shot himself. It was suicide."

I looked at him in surprise. "But we discarded the idea of suicide at the very beginning," I pointed out. "Why, it was you yourself who—"

"I was mistaken," he said coldly, annoyed that I should have mentioned it.

"But our original objections hold good," I pointed out. "Someone rang the doorbell and McNulty went to answer it. Professor Albrecht testified to that."

"Ah, but he didn't. We *thought* he did. What Albrecht actually said was that McNulty excused himself in the middle of their chess game with some remark about there being someone at the door. Here, let's go over the whole business and you'll see how we made our mistake. Professor Albrecht's story was that he was playing chess with McNulty. I take it that's a common thing with them."

"That's right," I said, "they play every Wednesday night, just as Nicky and I do every Friday evening. They dine together at the University Club and then go on to McNulty's place."

"Well, they didn't this Wednesday," said Edwards. "Albrecht was detained by some work in the lab and went on out to McNulty's house afterwards. In any case, they were playing chess. You recall the arrangement of furniture in McNulty's study? Here, let me show you." He opened the briefcase he had brought with him and drew out a photograph of the study. It showed a book-lined room with an opening in the form of an arch leading to a corridor. The chess table had been set up near the middle of the room, just to the right of the arch. The photograph had evidently been taken from just below the chess table so that it clearly showed the chess game in progress, the captured men, black and white, lying intermixed on one side of the board.

He pointed to a chair that was drawn up to the chess table.

"This is where Albrecht was sitting," Edwards explained, "facing the arch which is the entrance from the corridor. The vestibule and the front door beyond is down the corridor to the left—that is, Albrecht's left from where he was sitting.

"Now, his story was that in the middle of the game McNulty went to answer the door. Albrecht heard what he later decided was a pistol shot, but which at the time he thought was a car backfiring outside. That's reasonable because the evidence shows that the gun was pressed tightly against McNulty's body. That would muffle the sound, like firing into a pillow. In any case, Albrecht waited a couple of minutes and then called out. Receiving no answer, he went out to investigate and found his friend lying on the floor of the vestibule, shot through the heart, the still warm gun in his hand." He addressed himself to me. "Is that the way Albrecht told it? Did I leave out anything?"

I shook my head, wondering what was coming.

He smiled with great satisfaction. "Naturally, on the basis of that story we immediately ruled out suicide. We assumed that the man who rang the doorbell had shot him, and then thinking that McNulty was alone, had put the gun in his hand to make it look like suicide. If the doorbell rang, it had to be murder and could not be suicide. That's logical," he insisted firmly as though still annoyed that I had attributed the discarding of the suicide theory to him. "Even if the man who rang the doorbell had been a total stranger inquiring the way to the railroad station, say, it still could not have been suicide because it would have happened almost before the stranger could shut the door behind him and he would immediately have opened it again to see what the trouble was. It would have meant that McNulty had a loaded gun in his pocket all the time that he was playing chess with Albrecht. It would have meant—"

"All right," I interrupted, "the suicide theory was untenable. What made you change your mind?"

He showed some annoyance at my interruption, but suppressed it immediately. "The doorbell," he said solemnly. "There was something about Albrecht's story that didn't quite click. I took him over it several times. And then it came to me that at no time did he say that he had *heard* the doorbell—only that McNulty had excused himself with some remark about someone at the door. When I asked him point-blank if he had heard the bell, he became confused and finally admitted that he hadn't. He tried to explain it by saying that he was absorbed in the game, but it's a loud bell and if it had rung, I was sure he would have heard it. And since he didn't hear it, that meant it hadn't rung." He shrugged his shoulders. "Of course, if there were no third person at the door, the suicide theory had to be considered again."

He broke off suddenly. He blushed a little. "You know," he said in great earnestness, "I haven't been completely frank with you. I'm afraid I misled you into thinking that I came down here solely to investigate McNulty's death. The fact of the matter is that I arrived in the morning and made an appointment by phone to meet him at his home at half-past eight that night. You see, the research project on which McNulty and Albrecht have been working hasn't been going too well. There were strange mishaps occurring all too frequently. Delicate apparatus that would take weeks and months to replace was damaged. Reports had been late coming in and frequently contained errors. Army Ordinance which was sponsoring the project asked us to check on the work and I was sent down to make the preliminary investigation.

"Having in mind now the possibility of suicide, I asked Albrecht about sabotage on the project. That broke it. He admitted that he had been suspicious of McNulty for some time and had conducted a little investigation of his own. Though he was certain that McNulty was guilty, he had hesitated to accuse him openly. But he had hinted. All through the game he had hinted that he knew what McNulty had been up to. I gathered that he couched his hints in the terms of the game. I don't play chess, but I imagine that he said something like, 'You will be in great danger if you continue on this line'—that kind of thing. After a while, McNulty got the idea and became very upset. Albrecht said he murmured over and over again, 'What shall I do?' Then Albrecht made a move and said, 'Resign!'—which I understand is the regular chess term for 'give up.' " Edwards spread his hands as though presenting us with the case all nicely gift-wrapped. "It was then that McNulty muttered something about there being someone at the door and got up from the table."

"Albrecht saw him shoot himself?" I demanded.

"All but. He saw McNulty go through the arch. Instead of going to the left to the vestibule, he went to the right, and that's where his bedroom is. I submit that he went to get his gun. Then he came back and walked past the arch to the vestibule."

"Why didn't he wait until after Albrecht left?" I asked.

"I suppose because he knew that I would be along presently."

There was little doubt in my mind that Edwards had arrived at the correct solution. But I hated to admit it. It was no longer a question of beating Edwards to the finish. I was thinking of McNulty now. He was not a friend, but I had played chess with him at the University Club a number of times. I had not cared too much for the man, but I did not like to think of him taking his own life, especially since it implied that he had been guilty of treason. I suppose my uneasiness and my doubts were patent in the very vehemence with which I tried to conceal them. "And that's your case?" I demanded scornfully. "Why, a freshman law student could pick it to pieces! It's as full of holes as a sieve."

He reddened, a little taken aback at the belligerence in my tone.

"Such as?" he asked.

"Such as the gun? Have you traced it to him? Such as why did Albrecht lie in the first place? Such as the choice of the vestibule? Why should a man with a house full of rooms choose to shoot himself in the vestibule?"

"Albrecht lied because McNulty was his friend," Edwards replied. "He could no longer affect the research project—why should he make him out a suicide and a traitor if he could avoid it? Besides, I guess he felt a little guilty about McNulty's taking his own life. Remember? He called on him to resign. I imagine he must have been pretty upset to find that his friend took his advice so thoroughly."

"And the gun?"

Edwards shrugged his shoulders. "You yourself pointed out that the gun was a war trophy. The country is flooded with them and very few of them have been registered. A former student might have given it to him. As a matter of fact, Albrecht admitted that McNulty had mentioned something of the sort some months back. No, the gun didn't bother me. I found the business of the vestibule a lot harder to understand—until I made a thorough check of the house. It appears that since the death of his wife some years ago, McNulty has practically closed up all the upper part of the house and part of the lower. So although there are six rooms in the house, he actually occupies what amounts to a small apartment on the first floor consisting of the study which was formerly the dining room, a bedroom, and the kitchen. He couldn't shoot himself in the study since Albrecht was there and would stop him. The kitchen leads off the study and I suppose he would not want to pass Albrecht if he could help it. That leaves only the bedroom, which I would consider the most likely place were it not for one thing: there's a large portrait of his wife hanging there. It was taken full view so that the eyes seem to follow you no matter from what angle you look at it. It occurred to me that it was that which deterred him. He wouldn't want to shoot himself under the very eyes of his wife, as it were. That's only a guess, of course," he added with something of a smirk which implied that in his opinion it was a pretty good guess.

"It's a theory," I admitted grudgingly, "but it's no more than that. You have no proof."

"As a matter of fact," he said slowly, a malicious little smile playing about the corners of his mouth, "I have proof—absolute proof. We're pretty thorough in the Army and some of us have had quite a bit of experience. You see, I did a paraffin test on McNulty—and it was positive."

I should have known that he had an ace up his sleeve. This time I made no effort to conceal my disappointment. My shoulders drooped and I nodded slowly.

"What's a paraffin test?" asked Nicky, speaking for the first time.

"It's quite conclusive, Nicky," I said. "I'm not sure that I know the chemistry of it exactly, but it's scientifically correct. You see, every gun no matter how well fitted has a certain amount of backfire. Some of the gunpowder flashes back and is embedded in the hand of the man that fires. They coat his hand with hot paraffin and then draw it off like a glove. They then test it for gunpowder—for nitrates, that is—and if it's positive, it means that the man fired the gun. I'm afraid that winds it up for McNulty."

"So the oracle of the test tube has spoken?" Nicky murmured ironically.

"It's conclusive evidence, Nicky," I said.

"Evidence, eh? I was wondering when you would begin to examine the evidence," he remarked.

Edwards and I both looked at him, puzzled.

"What evidence have I neglected?" asked Edwards superciliously.

"Look at the photograph of the room," Nicky replied. "Look at that chess game."

I studied the photograph while Edwards watched uncertainly. It was not easy to see the position of the pieces because the ones nearest the camera were naturally greatly foreshortened. But after a moment I got the glimmering of an idea.

"Let's see what it looks like set up," I said, as I dumped the chessmen out of the box onto the table and then proceeded to select the necessary pieces to copy the position indicated in the photograph.

Nicky watched, a sardonic smile on his lips, amused at my inability to read the position directly from the photograph. Edwards looked uneasily from one to the other of us, half expecting to find the name of the murderer spelled out on the board.

"If there is some sort of clue in those chessmen," he essayed, "in the way they're set up, I mean, we can always check the position against the original. Nothing was moved and the house is sealed."

I nodded impatiently as I studied the board. The pattern of the pieces was beginning to take on a meaning in my mind. Then I had it.

"Why, he was playing the Logan-Asquith Gambit," I exclaimed. "And playing it extremely well."

"Never heard of it," said Nicky.

"Neither had I until McNulty showed it to me about a week ago at the University Club. He had come across it in Lowenstein's *End Games*. It's almost never used because it's such a risky opening. But it's interesting because of the way the position of the bishops is developed. Were you thinking, Nicky, that a man who was upset and about to shoot himself would not be playing so difficult a game, nor playing it so well?"

"As a matter of fact, I was thinking not of the position of the pieces on the board," said Nicky mildly, "but of those *off the board*—the captured men."

"What about them?" I demanded.

"They're all together on one side of the board, black and white."

"Well?"

Nicky's face was resigned, not to say martyred, and his tone was weary as he strove to explain what he thought should have been obvious.

"You play chess the way you write, or handle a tennis racket. If you're right-handed, you move your pieces with your right hand, and you take off your opponent's pieces with your right hand, and you deposit them on the table to your right. When two right-handed players like McNulty and Albrecht are engaged, the game ends with the black pieces that White has captured at his right and diagonally across the board are the white pieces that Black has captured."

There flashed through my mind the image of Trowbridge as I had seen him that afternoon, awkwardly trying to light a cigarette with his left hand because his right arm hung in a black silk sling.

"When a left-handed player opposes a right-handed player," Nicky went on, almost as though he had read my mind, "the captured men are on the same side of the board —but, of course, they're separated, the black chessmen near White and the white chessmen near Black. They wouldn't be jumbled together the way they are in the photograph unless—"

I glanced down at the board which I had just set up.

Nicky nodded as he would to a stupid pupil who had managed to stumble onto the right answer. "That's right —not unless you've dumped them out of the box and then set up only the men you need in accordance with the diagram of an end game."

"Do you mean that instead of playing a regular game,

McNulty was demonstrating some special kind of opening?" asked Edwards. He struggled with the idea, his eyes abstracted as he tried to fit it into the rest of the picture. Then he shook his head. "It doesn't make sense," he declared. "What would be the point of Albrecht's saying that they were playing a game?"

"Try it with Albrecht," Nicky suggested. "Suppose it was Albrecht who set up the board?"

"Same objection," said Edwards. "What would be the point of lying about it?"

"No point," Nicky admitted, "if he set it up before McNulty was shot. But suppose Albrecht set up the game *after* McNulty was shot."

"Why would he do that?" demanded Edwards, his belligerence growing with his bewilderment.

Nicky gazed dreamily at the ceiling. "Because a game of chess partly played suggests first, that the player has been there for some time, at least since the beginning of the game, and second, that he was there on friendly terms. It is hardly necessary to add that if a deliberate attempt is made to suggest both ideas, the chances are that neither is actually true."

"You mean—"

"I mean," said Nicky, "that Professor Luther Albrecht rang McNulty's doorbell at approximately eight o'clock and when McNulty opened the door for him, he pressed a gun against his breast and pulled the trigger, after which he put the gun in the dead man's hand and then stepped over his fallen body and coolly set up the ever-present chessmen in accordance with the diagram of an end game from one of McNulty's many books on chess. That's why the game was so well played. It had been worked out by an expert, by Lowenstein probably in the book you mentioned."

We both, the Colonel and I, sat back and just stared at Nicky. Edwards was the first to recover.

"But why should Albrecht shoot him? He was his best friend."

Nicky's little blue eyes glittered with amusement. "I suspect that you're to blame for that, Colonel. You called in the morning and made an appointment for that evening. I fancy that was what upset McNulty so. I doubt if he was directly to blame for the difficulties encountered on the project, but as head of the project he was responsible. I fancy that he told his good friend and colleague, Albrecht, about your call. And Albrecht knew that an investigation by an outsider meant certain discovery—unless he could provide a scapegoat, or what's the slang expression?—a fall guy, that's it, a fall guy."

I glanced at Edwards and saw that he was pouting like a small boy with a broken balloon. Suddenly he remembered something. His eyes lit up and his lips parted in a smile that was almost a sneer.

"It's all very pretty," he said, "but it's a lot of hogwash just the same. You've forgotten that I have proof that it was suicide. The paraffin test proved that McNulty had fired the gun."

Nicky smiled. "It's your test that is hogwash, Colonel. In this case it proves nothing."

"No, really," I intervened. "The test is perfectly correct."

"The test proves only that McNulty's hand was behind the gun," said Nicky sharply.

"Well?"

"Suppose someone rang your doorbell," Nicky addressed me, the same martyred look in his face, "as the Colonel did this evening, and when you opened the door, he thrust a gun against your breast. What would you do?"

"Why, I—I'd grab his hand, I suppose."

"Precisely, and if he fired at that instant, there would be nitrates backfired into your hand as well as into his."

The Colonel sat bolt upright. Then he jumped up and grabbed his briefcase and made for the door.

"You can't wash that stuff off too easily," he said over his shoulder. "And it's even harder to get it off your clothes. I'm going to get hold of Albrecht and do a paraffin on him."

When I returned to the study from seeing the Colonel to the door, Nicky said, "There was really no need for our young friend's haste. I could have offered him other proof—the chessmen. I have no doubt that the last fingerprint made on each chessman, black as well as white, will be found to be Albrecht's. And that would be a hard thing for him to explain if he persists in his story that it was just an ordinary game of chess."

"Say, that's right, Nicky. I'll spring that one on Edwards in the morning." I hesitated, then I took the plunge. "Wasn't Albrecht taking an awful chance though? Wouldn't it have been better if he had just walked away after shooting McNulty instead of staying on and calling the police and making up that story and—"

Nicky showed his exasperation. "Don't you see it? He couldn't walk off. The poor devil was stuck there. He had got McNulty's lifeless hand nicely fitted onto the gun. He was ready to leave. Naturally, he looked through the door window up and down the street, normally deserted at that hour, to make sure the coast was clear. And he saw Trowbridge trudging along. He waited a minute or two for him to pass and then looked out again only to find that the young man had stopped directly across the street and gave no indication of moving on. And in a minute or two the passengers from the Albany train would be along. And after that, perhaps our friend the Colonel, early for his appointment."

"So my investigation of Trowbridge wasn't entirely fruitless, eh?" I exclaimed, rubbing my hands together gleefully. "At least, that puts me one up on the Colonel."

Nicky nodded. "A brash young man, that. What branch of the service did he say he was connected with?"

"Intelligence."

"Indeed!" Nicky pursed his lips and then relaxed them in a frosty little smile. "I was infantry, myself, in the last war."

Time and Time Again

ALTHOUGH it was more than two years since I had left the Law Faculty to become County Attorney, I still maintained some connection with the university. I still had the privileges of the gymnasium and the library and I still kept up my membership in the Faculty Club. I dropped in there occasionally for a game of billiards, and about once a month I dined there, usually with Nicholas Welt.

We had finished dinner, Nicky and I, and had repaired to the Commons Room for a game of chess, only to find that all the tables were in use. So we joined the group in front of the fire where there was always interminable talk about such highly scholarly matters as to whether there was any likelihood of favorable action by the trustees on an increase in salary schedules—there wasn't—or whether you got more miles per gallon with a Chevrolet than you got with a Ford.

This evening as we joined the group, the talk was about Professor Rollins' paper in the *Quarterly Journal* of *Psychic Research* which no one had read but on which everyone had an opinion. The title of the paper was something like "Modifications in the Sprague Method of Analysis of Extra-Sensory Experimentation Data," but the academic mind with its faculty for generalization had quickly gone beyond the paper and Rollins' theories to a discussion on whether there was anything in "this business of the supernatural," with burly Professor Lionel Graham, Associate in Physics, asserting that "of course, there couldn't be when you considered the type of people who went in for it, gypsies and what not." And gentle, absentminded Roscoe Summers, Professor of Archaeology, maintaining doggedly that you couldn't always tell by that and that he had heard stories from people whose judgment he respected that made you pause and think a bit.

To which Professor Graham retorted, "That's just the trouble. It's always something that happened to somebody else. Or better still, something that somebody told you that happened to somebody *he* knew." Then catching sight of us, he said, "Isn't that right, Nicky? Did you ever hear about anything supernatural as having happened to somebody you yourself knew well and whose word and opinion you could rely on?"

Nicky's lined, gnomelike face relaxed in a frosty little smile. "I'm afraid that's how I get most of my information," he said. "I mean through hearing about it at third or fourth hand."

Dr. Chisholm, the young instructor in English Composition, had been trying to get a word in and now he succeeded. "I had a case last summer. I mean I was there and witnessed something that was either supernatural or was a most remarkable coincidence."

"Something on the stage, or was it a seance in a dark room?" asked Graham with a sneer.

"Neither," said Chisholm defiantly. "I saw a man cursed and he died of it." He caught sight of a pompous little man with a shining bald head and he called out, "Professor Rollins, won't you join us? I'm sure you'd be interested in a little incident I was about to tell."

Professor Rollins, the author of the paper in the *Quarterly,* approached and the men sitting on the red leather divan moved over respectfully to make room for him. But he seemed to sense that he was being asked to listen as an expert and he selected a straight-backed chair as being more in keeping with the judicial role he was to play.

I spent my summer vacation (Chisholm began) in a little village on the Maine coast. It was not a regular summer resort and there was little to do all day long except sit on the rocks and watch the gulls as they swooped above the water. But I had worked hard all year and it was precisely what I wanted.

The center of the town was inland, clustered about the little railroad depot, and I was fortunate in getting a room way out at the end of town near the water. My host was a man named Doble, a widower in his forties, a decent quiet man who was good company when I wanted company and who did not obtrude when I just wanted to sit and daydream. He did a little farming and had some chickens; he had a boat and some lobster pots; and for the rest, he'd make a little money at various odd jobs. He didn't work by the day but would contract for the whole job which put him a cut above the ordinary odd jobman, I suppose.

Ours was the last house on the road and our nearest neighbor was about a hundred yards away. It was a large nineteenth century mansion, set back from the road, and decorated with the traditional fretsaw trim and numerous turrets and gables. It was owned and occupied by Cyrus Cartwright, the president of the local bank and the richest man in town.

He was a brisk, eager sort of man, like the advertisement for a correspondence course in salesmanship, the type of man who carries two watches and is always glancing at his wristwatch and then checking it against his pocket watch.

(Chisholm warmed as he described Cyrus Cartwright, the result of the natural antipathy of a man who spends his summer watching sea gulls for the type of man who weighs out his life in small minutes. Now he smiled disarmingly and shrugged his shoulders.)

I saw him only once. I had come in town with Doble and before going home, he stopped in at the bank to see if Cartwright was still interested in making some change in the electric wiring system in his house which they had talked about some months ago. It was typical of Doble that he should only now be coming around to make further inquiry about it.

Cartwright glanced at the radium dial of his wristwatch and then tugged at his watch chain and drew out his pocket watch, squeezing it out of its protective chamois covering. He mistook my interest in the ritual for interest in the watch itself and held it out so that I could see it, explaining with some condescension that it was a repeater, a five-minute repeater he was at some pains to point out, and then proceeded to demonstrate it by pressing a catch so that I could hear it tinkle the hour and then in a different key tinkle once for every five-minute interval after the hour.

I made some comparison between the man who carries two watches and the man who wears both a belt and suspenders. But though he realized I was joking, he said with some severity, "Time is money, sir, and I like to know just where I am with both. So I keep accurate books and accurate watches."

Having put me in my place, he turned to Doble and said crisply, "I don't think I'll bother with it, Doble. It was Jack's idea having the extra light and switch in the hallway and now that he's gone into the service, I don't think I'll need it. When it gets dark, I go to bed."

Once again he glanced at his wristwatch, checked its accuracy against his pocket watch as before, and then he smiled at us, a short, meaningless, businessman's smile of dismissal.

As I say, I saw him only that once, but I heard a great deal about him. You know how it is, you hear a man's name mentioned for the first time and then it seems to pop up again and again in the next few days.

According to Doble, Cartwright was a tight-fisted old skinflint who had remained a bachelor, probably to save the expense of supporting a wife.

When I pointed out that paying a housekeeper to come in every day was almost as expensive as keeping a wife, and that in addition he had brought up his nephew

Jack, Doble retorted that nobody but Mrs. Knox would take the job of Cartwright's housekeeper and that she took it only because no one else would take her. She was almost stone deaf and general opinion was that her wages were small indeed.

"As for Jack," he went on, "the old man never let him see a penny more than he actually needed. He never had a dime in his pocket, and when he'd go into town of an evening, he'd just have to hang around—usually didn't even have the price of a movie. Nice young fellow too," he added reflectively.

"He could have got a job and left," I suggested.

"I suppose he could've," Doble said slowly, "but he's the old man's heir, you see, and I guess he figured it was kind of politic, as you might say, to hang around doing any little jobs at the bank that the old man might ask of him."

I was not too favorably impressed with the young man's character from Doble's description, but I changed my mind when he came down a few days later on furlough.

He turned out to be a decent chap, quiet and reserved, but with a quick and imaginative mind. We grew quite close in those few days and saw a great deal of each other. We went fishing off the rocks, or lazed around in the sun a good deal talking of all sorts of things, or shot at chips in the water with an old rifle that he had.

He kept his gun and fishing rod over at our house. And that gives some indication of the character of Cyrus Cartwright and of Jack's relations with him. He explained that his uncle knew that he wasn't doing anything during this week of furlough and didn't really expect him to, but if he saw him with the fishing rod, that traditional symbol of idleness, it would seem as though he were flaunting his indolence in his face. As for the gun, Cyrus Cartwright considered shooting at any target that could not subsequently be eaten as an extravagant waste of money for shells.

Jack came over every evening to play cribbage or perhaps to sit on the porch and sip at a glass of beer and argue about some book he had read at my suggestion. Sometimes he spoke about his uncle and in discussing him, he was not bitter—ironic, rather.

On one occasion he explained, "My uncle is a good man according to his lights. He likes money because it gives him a sense of accomplishment to have more than anyone else in town. But that alone doesn't make him a hard person to live with. What does make him difficult is that everything is set in a rigid routine, a senseless routine, and his household has to conform to it. After dinner, he sits and reads his paper until it gets dark. Then he looks at his wristwatch and shakes his head a little as though he didn't believe it was that late. Then he takes his pocket watch out and checks the wristwatch against it. But of course, even that doesn't satisfy him. So he goes into the dining room where he has an electric clock and he sets both watches by that.

"When he's got all timepieces perfectly synchronized, he says, 'Well, it's getting late,' and he goes upstairs to his room. In about fifteen minutes he calls to me and I go up to find him already in bed.

" 'I forgot to fix the windows,' he says. So I open them

an inch at the top and an inch at the bottom. It takes a bit of doing because if I should open them a quarter of an inch too wide, he says he'll catch his death of cold, and if it is short of an inch, he's sure he'll smother. But finally I get them adjusted just right and he says, 'My watch, would you mind, Jack?' So I get his pocket watch that he had put on the bureau while undressing and I put it on the night table near his bed.

"As far back as I can remember, I've had to do that little chore. I am sure he insists on it so as to fix our relations in my mind. While I was away, he must have remembered to do it for himself, but the first day I got back I had to do it."

(Chisholm looked from one to the other of us as if to make sure that we all understood the characters and their relations with each other. I nodded encouragingly and he continued.)

Jack was scheduled to leave Sunday morning and naturally we expected to see him Saturday, but he did not show up during the day. He came over in the evening, after dinner, however, and he was hot and angry.

"The hottest day of the summer," he exclaimed, "and today of all days my uncle suddenly finds a bunch of errands for me to do. I've been all over the county and I couldn't even take the car. I'll bet you fellows were lying out on the beach all day. How about going in for a dip right now?"

Well, of course, we had been in and out of the water all day long, but it was still hot and muggy, and besides we could see that he wanted very much to go, so we agreed. We took some beer down and we didn't bother with bathing suits since it was already quite dark. After a while, however, it began to get chilly. It had clouded up and the air was oppressive as though a storm were impending. So we got dressed again and went back to our house.

The atmosphere had a charged, electric quality about it, and whether it was that or because he was leaving the following day, Jack was unusually quiet and conversation lagged. Around half past eleven, he rose and stretched and said he thought he ought to be going.

"It's been good meeting you," he said. "I didn't look forward to this furlough particularly, but now I'm sure I'm going to look back on it."

We shook hands and he started for the door. Then he remembered about his fishing rod and his rifle and came back for them. He seemed reluctant to leave us, and Doble, understanding, said, "We might as well walk down with you, Jack."

He nodded gratefully and all three of us strolled out into the darkness. We walked along slowly, Jack with his fishing rod over one shoulder and his gun over the other.

I offered to carry the gun, but he shook his head and handed me the rod instead. I took it and walked on in silence until we reached the gate of his uncle's house. Perhaps he misinterpreted my silence and felt that he had been ungracious, for he said, "I'm a lot more used to carrying a rifle than you are." And then lest I take his remark as a reflection on my not being in the service, he hurried on with, "I'm kind of fond of this gun. I've had it a long time and had a lot of fun with it."

He patted the stock affectionately like a boy with a

dog and then he nestled the butt against his shoulder and sighted along the barrel.

"Better not, Jack," said Doble with a grin. "You'll wake your uncle."

"Damn my uncle," he retorted lightly, and before we could stop him, he pulled the trigger.

In that silence, the crack of the rifle was like a thunderclap. I suppose we all expected one of the windows to fly up and the irate voice of old Cartwright to demand what was going on. In any case, instinctively, like three small boys, we all ducked down behind the fence where we could not be seen. We waited several minutes, afraid to talk lest we be overheard. But when nothing happened, we straightened up slowly and Doble said, "You better get to bed, Jack. I think maybe you've had a little too much beer."

"Maybe I ought at that," Jack answered and eased the gate open.

Then he turned and whispered, "Say, do you fellows mind waiting a minute? I think I may have locked the door and I haven't a key."

We nodded and watched as he hurried down the path to the house. Just before he reached the door, however, he hesitated, stopped, and then turned and came hurrying back to us.

"Could you put me up for the night, Doble?" he asked in a whisper.

"Why sure, Jack. Was the door locked?"

He didn't answer immediately and we started down the road to our house. We had gone about halfway when he said, "I didn't check to see if the door was locked or not."

"I noticed that," I remarked.

There was another silence and then as we mounted the porch steps, the moon, which had been hidden by clouds, suddenly broke through and I saw that he was deathly pale.

"What's the matter, Jack?" I asked quickly.

He shook his head and did not answer. I put my hand on his arm and asked again, "Are you all right?"

He nodded and tried to smile.

"I've—I've— Something funny happened to me," he said. "Did you mean what you said the other day about believing in spirits?"

At first I could not think what he was referring to, and then I remembered having argued—not too seriously—for belief in the supernatural during a discussion of William Blake's *Marriage of Heaven and Hell* which I had lent him.

I shrugged my shoulders noncommittally, wondering what he was getting at.

He smiled wanly. "I didn't really have too much beer," he said and looked at me for confirmation.

"No, I don't think you did," I said quietly.

"Look," he went on, "I'm cold sober. And I was sober a few minutes ago when I started for my uncle's house. But as I came near the door, I felt something like a cushion of air building up against me to block my progress. And then, just before I reached the door, it became so strong that I could not go on. It was like a wall in front of me. But it was something more than an inanimate wall. It did not merely block me, but seemed to be pushing me back as though it had a will and intelligence like a strong man. It frightened me and I turned back. I'm still frightened."

"Your uncle—" I began.

"Damn my uncle!" he said vehemently. "I hope he falls and breaks his neck."

Just then Doble's kitchen clock chimed twelve. The brassy ring, coming just as he finished, seemed to stamp the curse with fateful approval.

It made us all a little uncomfortable. We didn't seem to feel like talking, and after a while we went to bed.

We were awakened the next morning early by someone pounding on the door. Doble slipped his trousers on and I managed to get into my bathrobe. We reached the front door about the same time. It was Mrs. Knox, Cartwright's housekeeper, and she was in a state of considerable excitement.

"Mister Cartwright's dead!" she shouted to us. "There's been an accident."

Since she was deaf, it was no use to question her. We motioned her to wait while we put on our shoes. Then we followed her back to the house. The front door was open as she had left it when she had hurried over to us. And from the doorway we could see the figure of Cyrus Cartwright in an old-fashioned nightgown, lying at the foot of the stairs, his head in a sticky pool of blood.

He was dead all right, and looking up we could see the bit of rumpled carpeting at the head of the stairs which had probably tripped him up and catapulted him down the long staircase.

He had died as he had lived, for in his right hand he still clutched his precious pocket watch. The watch he was wearing on his wrist, however, had smashed when he fell and it gave us the time of his death. The hands pointed to just before twelve, the exact time as near as I could judge, that Jack had uttered his curse!

There was a minute of appreciative silence after Chisholm finished. I could see that no one's opinion had been changed materially by the story. Those who had been skeptical were scornful now and those who were inclined to believe, were triumphant, but we all turned to Professor Rollins to see what he thought and he was nodding his head portentously.

Nicky, however, was the first to speak. "And the pocket watch," he said, "Had that stopped, too?"

"No, that was ticking away merrily," Chisholm replied. "I guess his hand must have cushioned it when he fell. It had probably been badly jarred though, because it was running almost an hour ahead."

Nicky nodded grimly.

"What about Jack? How did he take it?" I asked.

Chisholm considered for a moment. "He was upset naturally, not so much over his uncle's death, I fancy, since he did not care for him very much, but because of the fact that it confirmed his fears of the night before that some supernatural influence was present." He smiled sadly. "I did not see him much after that. He had got his leave extended, but he was busy with his uncle's affairs. When finally he went back to the Army, he promised to write, but he never did. Just last week, however, I got a letter from Doble. He writes me occasionally—just the usual gossip of the town. In his letter he mentions that Jack Cartwright crashed in his first solo flight."

"Ah." Professor Rollins showed interest. "I don't mind admitting that I rather expected something like that."

"You expected Jack to die?" Chisholm asked in amazement.

Rollins nodded vigorously. "This was truly a supernatural manifestation. I haven't the slightest doubt about it. For one thing, Jack felt the supernatural forces. And the curse, followed almost immediately by its fulfillment even to the manner of death, that is most significant. Now, of course we know very little of these things, but we suspect that they follow a definite pattern. Certain types of supernatural forces have what might be called an ironic bent, a sort of perverted sense of humor. To be sure, when Jack uttered his fervent wish that his uncle fall and break his neck, he was speaking as a result of a momentary exasperation, but it is the nature of evil or mischievous forces to grant just such wishes. We meet with it again and again in folklore and fairy tales, which are probably the cryptic or symbolic expression of the wisdom of the folk. The pattern is familiar to you all, I am sure, from the stories of your childhood. The wicked character is granted three wishes by a fairy, only to waste them through wishes that are just such common expressions of exasperation as Jack used. You see, when supernatural forces are present, a mere wish, fervently expressed, may serve to focus them, as it were. And that is what happened at the Cartwright house that fateful evening."

He held up a forefinger to ward off the questions that leaped to our minds.

"There is another element in the pattern," he went on soberly, "and that is that whenever a person does profit materially through the use of evil supernatural forces, even though unintentionally on his part, sooner or later, they turn on him and destroy him. I have no doubt that Jack's death was just as much the result of supernatural forces as was the death of his uncle."

Professor Graham muttered something that sounded like "Rubbish."

Dana Rollins, who could have gone on indefinitely I suppose, stopped abruptly and glared.

But Professor Graham was not one to be silenced by a look. "The young man died as a result of a plane crash. Well, so did thousands of others. Had they all been granted three wishes by a wicked fairy? Poppycock! The young man died because he went up in a plane. That's reason enough. As for the old man, he tumbled down the stairs and cracked his skull or broke his neck, whichever it was. You say his nephew's curse must have been uttered about the same time. Well, even granting that by some miracle Doble's kitchen clock was synchronized to Cartwright's watches, that would still be nothing more than a coincidence. The chances are that the young man uttered that same wish hundreds of times. It was only natural: he was his heir and besides, he didn't like him. Now on one of those hundreds of times, it actually happened. There's nothing supernatural in that—not even anything out of the ordinary. It makes a good story, young man, but it doesn't prove anything."

"And Jack's sensing of a supernatural force," asked Chisholm icily, "is that just another coincidence?"

Graham shrugged his massive shoulders. "That was probably just an excuse not to go home. He was probably afraid he'd get a dressing down from his uncle for shooting off his rifle in the middle of the night. What do you think, Nicky?"

Nicky's little blue eyes glittered. "I rather think," he said, "that the young man was not so much afraid of his uncle asking him about the rifle as he was that he would ask him what time it was."

We all laughed at Nicky's joke. But Professor Graham was not to be put off.

"Seriously, Nicky," he urged.

"Well then, seriously," said Nicky with a smile as though he were indulging a bright but impetuous freshman, "I think you're quite right in calling the young man's death an accident. Parenthetically, I might point out that Dr. Chisholm did not suggest that it was anything else. As for the uncle's death, I cannot agree with you that it was merely coincidence."

Professor Rollins pursed his lips and appeared to be considering Nicky's cavalier dismissal of half his theory, but it was obvious that he was pleased at his support for the other half. I could not help reflecting how Nicky automatically assumed control over any group that he found himself in. He had a way of treating people, even his colleagues on the faculty, as though they were immature schoolboys. And curiously, people fell into this role that he assigned to them.

Professor Graham, however, was not yet satisfied. "But dammit all, Nicky," he insisted, "a man trips on a bit of carpet and falls downstairs. What is there unusual about that?"

"In the first place, I think it is unusual that he should

go downstairs at all," said Nicky. "Why do you suppose he did?"

Professor Graham looked at him in aggrieved surprise like a student who has just been asked what he considers an unfair question.

"How should I know why he went downstairs?" he said. "I suppose he couldn't sleep and wanted a snack, or maybe a book to read."

"And took his pocket watch with him?"

"Well, according to Chisholm he was always checking his wristwatch against it."

Nicky shook his head. "When you're wearing two watches, it's almost impossible not to check the other after you've glanced at the one, just as we automatically glance at our watches when we pass the clock in the jeweler's window even though we might have set it by the radio only a minute or two before. But for Cyrus Cartwright to take his pocket watch downstairs with him when he had a watch on his wrist is something else again. I can think of only one reason for it."

"And what's that?" asked Chisholm curiously.

"To see what time it was on the electric clock."

I could understand something of Graham's exasperation as he exclaimed, "But dammit, Nicky, the man had two watches. Why would he want to go downstairs to see the time?"

"Because in this case, two watches were not as good as one," said Nicky quietly.

I tried to understand. Did he mean that the supernatural force that had manifested itself to Jack Cartwright that night and had prevented him from entering the house had somehow tampered with the watches?

"What was wrong with them?" I asked.

"They disagreed."

Then he leaned back in his chair and looked about him with an air of having explained everything. There was a short silence and as he scanned our faces, his expression of satisfaction changed to one of annoyance.

"Don't you see yet what happened?" he demanded. "When you wake up in the middle of the night, the first thing you do is look at the clock on the mantelpiece or your watch on the night table in order to orient yourself. That's precisely what Cyrus Cartwright did. He woke up and glancing at his wristwatch he saw that it was a quarter to twelve, say. Then quite automatically he reached for his pocket watch on the night table. He pressed the catch and the chiming mechanism tinkled twelve and then went on to tinkle half or three quarters past. He had set the watches only a few hours before and both of them were going, and yet one was about an hour faster than the other. Which was right? What time was it? I fancy he tried the repeater again and again and then tried to dismiss the problem from his mind until morning. But after tossing about for a few minutes, he realized that if he hoped to get back to sleep that night, he would have to go downstairs to see what time it really was." Nicky turned to Chisholm. "You see, the jar from the fall would not have moved the watch ahead. A blow will either stop the movement or it might speed up or slow down the escapement for a few seconds. But a watch with hands so loose that a jar will move them would be useless as a timepiece. Hence, the watch must have been moved ahead sometime before the fall. Cyrus Cartwright would not do it, which means that his nephew must have, probably while transferring the watch, from the bureau to the night table."

"You mean accidentally?" asked Chisholm. "Or to annoy his uncle?"

Nicky's little blue eyes glittered. "Not to annoy him," he said, "to murder him!"

He smiled pleasantly at our stupefaction. "Oh yes, no doubt about it," he assured us. "After arranging the windows to his uncle's satisfaction and placing the watch on the night table, Jack bade his uncle a courteous good night. And on his way out, he stopped just long enough to rumple or double over the bit of carpet at the head of the stairs. There was no light in the hallway remember."

"But—but I don't understand. I don't see—I mean, how did he know that his uncle was going to wake up in the middle of the night?" Chisholm finally managed.

"Firing off his rifle under his uncle's windows insured that, I fancy," Nicky replied. He smiled. "And now you can understand, I trust, why he could not enter his uncle's house that night. He was afraid that his uncle, awake now, would hear him come in and instead of venturing downstairs, would simply call down to him to ask what time it was."

This time we did not laugh.

The silence that followed was suddenly broken by the chiming of the chapel clock. Subconsciously, we glanced at our watches, and then realizing what we were doing, we all laughed.

"Quite," said Nicky.

The Whistling Tea Kettle

I WAS fully prepared to spend the week or ten days that it would take to redo my house at a hotel, but when I mentioned it to Nicky Welt and he suggested that I bunk in with him instead, I was curiously touched and readily accepted. He treated me as very much his junior, usually with a touch of condescension, as of the teacher for the not overbright sophomore, and I fell into the role assigned me. It had been that way from the beginning of our friendship when I had first joined the Law Faculty, and it continued even after I left teaching to campaign—successfully—for the office of County Attorney.

He lived in a boardinghouse a couple of blocks from the railroad depot at some little distance from the university, a circumstance which from his point of view was one of the virtues of the place since it gave him a brisk fifteen-minute constitutional every day, and also cut down on the number of people who might be likely to drop in on him of an evening had he been nearer. He occupied a small suite on the second floor consisting of bedroom, study, and bath, and either by reason of his seniority at the boardinghouse—he had lived there all the time I had known him—or by reason of his academic eminence, and in a university town that is important, he was the star boarder. Mrs. Keefe, the landlady, was always doing special little things for him, such as bringing up a tray with cake and coffee in the evening, and this in spite of his having an electric hot-plate in his room, as did all the rooms in the establishment, and quite able to do for himself. Obviously, she offered no objection to my coming there. In fact, it was all Nicky could do to prevent her from removing the cot in the study and bringing in a full-sized bed so that I would be more comfortable.

As it turned out, I was fortunate in the arrangement, for a portion of that period of ten days coincided with a university convocation. We had had convocations before, and they had disturbed the even flow of university life but little, but this year the university had a new president, one of the new type of college presidents, a young, eager, efficient executive, and he had arranged for scholars and big-wigs to be drawn from the ends of the earth. There were meetings and conferences and panel discussions scheduled for every hour for each of the three days. But what is more to the purpose, every hotel room in town, every bit of available dormitory space, seemingly every unoccupied bed had been commandeered by the university for the expected distinguished guests. If I had gone to a hotel, I probably would have had to share my room with one or more of the visitors. And if I had remained in my own house, I would have been in a worse case—the unwilling host of a dozen or more. As it was, Professor Richardson, who was Chairman of the Committee on Housing Arrangements, gave me a reproachful look when I ran across him at the Faculty Club, and practically implied that I had purposely arranged to have my house done over during Convocation Week just to avoid having to entertain the guests of the university.

Mrs. Keefe, on the other hand, like all the boarding-house proprietors, was naturally delighted. She had a room up in the attic which she rarely succeeded in renting, into which she now managed to crowd three young women from India who were to take part in the discussions on Village Medicine. She had coaxed or browbeaten the amiable young graduate student who had the room immediately above ours to sharing his room with a bearded Pakistani in a turban. The room across the hall from us was occupied by another graduate student who had been called home because of sickness in the family and she had promptly rented it, presumably with his permission, to two of the visitors, one of whom arrived Sunday and the other the following day by the evening train.

Later that evening, after the two men had had a chance to get settled, Nicky knocked on their door and invited them to spend the evening with us. I am sure that he was moved as much by curiosity as he was by natural feelings of hospitality. The earlier arrival was a young man of about thirty, tall and blond, with a charming mid-European accent and the impossible name of Erik Flugelheimer. He was lively and vivacious, and yet withal, he had a humility that was not the least part of his charm. His roommate was a short dark man, perhaps ten years older, whose name was Earl Blodgett. He was stuffy and pompous and quite convinced of his own importance. He turned out to be none other than the Assistant Curator of the Far East Division of the Laurence Winthrop Collection. Since the theme of the Convocation was, as the program leaflet gave it, "The New World of the Far East," his importance in the general scheme of things was obvious. He was also precise, and meticulous and crotchety.

When Nicky set about preparing coffee for our guests, Blodgett said, "I'm afraid I can't. It keeps me awake till all hours. Might I have some tea instead? Do you have a kettle? If not, I can get the one in our room."

Nicky assured him that he had tea and a kettle and was about to prepare it when he begged leave to prepare it himself. "I am very particular as to just how it is brewed. I'm sure you won't mind."

Nicky did mind, of course, but as host he was being gracious and he motioned his guest to the hot-plate.

Erik laughed. "He cannot abide coffee and I can't stand tea. We have both a teapot and a percolator but we have only one burner on our hot-plate. We shall have to toss a coin to decide who will make his drink first in the morning."

We sipped at our drinks and talked about the events that were scheduled. I remarked that the emphasis seemed to be primarily political and sociological and that for that reason there might not be too much interest in the Art Section meetings.

"I have every reason to believe," Blodgett said with lofty complacency, "that the Art Section will provide the most noteworthy contribution of the Convocation."

"Are you planning a surprise of some sort?" I asked.

Blodgett favored me with a superior smile. "Have you ever heard of the Adelphi Bowl?" he asked.

Nicky pricked up his ears. "George Slocumbe, he's the Fine Arts man here, was telling me about it the other day. He said it had recently been acquired by a private collection. He didn't mention the Laurence Winthrop Collection. Do you mean that you have it and are planning to exhibit it here?"

"What is it, Nicky?" I asked.

"It's a bowl made of massive gold and encrusted with precious stones. It's worth—"

"It is priceless," said Blodgett.

"And you are going to exhibit here at the Convocation?" I asked.

Blodgett shrugged his shoulders. "Perhaps."

Rather than press him, I turned to his roommate. "And you, are you going to surprise the Convocation, too?"

The blond young man shook his head ruefully. "I am not one of the distinguished scholars like my roommate who have been invited to read papers. I am an instructor of mathematics at Muhlbach College in North Dakota. Have you ever heard of it? Ah, I thought not. It is a small denominational college where once a year the Minneapolis Symphony gives a concert and maybe two or three times a year we get a road company with the New York hits of three years ago. So when notice of your convocation was posted on the bulletin board and I saw that it would come during our April vacation, I decided to come here. I shall attend as many sessions as I can. Who knows, I might get to ask an intelligent question and this might call me to the attention of one of your distinguished guests from one of the larger colleges who might decide that I might make a worthwhile addition to his faculty and rescue me from Muhlbach."

The Convocation was scheduled to last three days—Monday, Tuesday, and Wednesday. Blodgett's talk was scheduled for Wednesday evening. He chose to regard the scheduling as indicative of the importance of his talk, as though the Convocation was arranged to work up to a gradual climax. Under the circumstances, I did not have the heart to point out that since the evening train left about an hour before his discourse, the likelihood was that the great majority of the guests would have left the university by the time he was scheduled to speak since otherwise they would have to stay overnight until the next day before they could get a train out.

The next day, Tuesday, I left my office early, just after lunch in fact. It was too nice a day to work. I strolled along leisurely, savoring the April air. I chose the long way back to the boardinghouse—through the campus. I saw Earl Blodgett and stopped to talk with him. I invited him to join me back at the house, but he was planning to take in some of the lectures and I left him.

Just as I arrived at the boardinghouse, I saw Erik turn the corner. I waited for him and we walked up the front stairs together. The mail had just been delivered and was lying in a pile on the hall table. I riffled through the letters to see if there was anything for me or for Nicky.

"I don't suppose there is anything for me," Erik said.

"Here's one for your roommate though," and I handed him an envelope.

Included in the mail were a couple of magazines and

I glanced through them idly while Erik went on up to his room. Nicky was at his desk in the study correcting student blue books when I entered.

"Are you planning to go to the Convocation Dinner tonight?" I asked.

He gave me a sour grin. "I went to the Convocation Luncheon this noon," he said. "That's about as much Convocation as I can stand for a while. I can forgive the gelatinous creamed chicken in soggy pastry shell since that's standard, but the conversation at these affairs is a little more difficult on the digestion. There were two females, one on either side of me, who were conversing largely across me and talking the most utter drivel. One urged with all seriousness that mirrored in every leaf or bud there is the clue to the entire cosmos. I am not unfamiliar with the more insane theories of the transcendentalists, but I don't believe any of them ever really believed the nonsense as a purely practical matter; that is, that one could determine the speed of the earth's rotation by studying the leaf of a tree."

"And you think your luncheon companion did?"

"Well, she had been in India, and she had been taken to all the tourist traps—the usual guru, and this one's forte was to take a single hair from a man's head and tell all about him. Another thing that he did: he had himself blindfolded and he had one of the company—there were about twenty as I understand—pluck a single note on a native harp, and then he was able to tell which of the twenty had struck the note."

"That's rather hard to believe of course, but I once spoke to a concert pianist who told me that if he and Rubinstein both struck the same key on the same piano, there would be a distinct difference in sound that would be apparent to anyone."

"Nonsense," said Nicky decisively.

At that moment the quiet of our boardinghouse was broken by the shrill hoarse whistle of our neighbor's tea kettle. Nicky is so positive in his opinions that the chance of scoring on him was irresistible. I appeared to be listening intently for a moment, then I said, "I am not so sure, Nicky. Now I would be willing to wager that the discordant note of that tea kettle shows the fine Middle European hand of our friend Erik, rather than the restrained, repressed character of the excellent Blodgett."

"Then you would lose," said Nicky with a wry grin, "Because it is Earl Blodgett who is the tea drinker; Erik drinks coffee."

I rattled the loose coins in my trouser pocket. "I am still willing to make the wager," I said smugly.

Nicky peered at me out from under his bushy eyebrows. "You are too certain," he said. "You must know something. Did you meet Erik on the stairs and did he tell you that his roommate was not in?"

I nodded sheepishly. "Something like that. I met Earl at the university and he said he was staying for some lectures. Erik came in with me. I stopped to look through the mail. There was a letter for Earl which I gave him to take up. I assumed that Earl didn't change his mind about the lectures and that Erik must be in the room alone. I suppose he decided to try the tea for once just to see what Earl finds in the stuff."

Nicky had turned back to his blue books even while I was talking. Without looking up, he said, "The whistling of the tea kettle does not mean that our friend is brewing tea, only that he is boiling water."

"What else would he boil water for?"

"There are any number of reasons he might have for boiling water. He might even be interested not in the water but in the by-product."

"What's the by-product of boiling water?" I demanded.

"Steam."

"Steam? What would he want with steam?"

Nicky put his pile of blue books away and looked up at me. "He might want it for loosening the gummed flap on an envelope."

"You think he is opening Blodgett's letter? Why would he want to read Blodgett's mail?"

Nicky sat back in his chair. "Let's think about it. Of course he might be an extremely inquisitive person who finds anything that is closed to him a challenge to his curiosity. But that's not too likely. It is also most unlikely that he knows anyone who would be apt to be writing to Blodgett. That suggests that there was something about the sealed envelope that indicated that it would be worth his while to open it."

I fell into the spirit of the game. "You mean he could tell something from the handwriting or the return address?"

"That's a possibility," said Nicky, "but it would mean that the address was in Blodgett's own handwriting."

"How do you arrive at that conclusion?"

"Well, consider, the two men, Blodgett and Erik, are engaged in entirely different fields of study; they come from utterly different backgrounds, and from widely separate parts of the country. It is most unlikely that they have any friends or acquaintances in common. The only handwriting that he might be familiar with would be Blodgett's, from having seen his notes lying about perhaps. It is possible that that might excite his curiosity: what is Blodgett writing to himself? But what I had in mind was that the mere feel of the envelope might lead him to want to open it."

"Money? You mean it might contain money—bills of large denomination?"

Nicky shook his head. "They would feel just like any other paper. If it were something heavy—"

"Like a coin," I exclaimed, having in mind a rare antique.

"Possible, but not reasonable. If it were a coin of great value, he would be fairly certain to see it when Blodgett opened his letter—if he only wanted to see it. On the other hand, if he wanted to steal it, he would not bother to steam the envelope open, he would merely take it. Sooner or later, however, the theft would be discovered and investigation would prove that Erik must have taken it. No, I would say that that line of reasoning is not too fertile. I am inclined to agree that the envelope contained something that could be felt, probably metal, necessarily flat. But I rather think that it would be something that has no great value in itself, a key for instance."

"A woman—"

Nicky smiled. "You are incurably romantic. You were about to suggest that some woman had sent Blodgett a key to her apartment for an assignation. Somehow our friend Blodgett doesn't seem the type. And why would Erik be interested in his roommate's amours? No, no, a locker key is more likely than a house key." Nicky nodded his head vigorously. "Yes, a locker key is the most likely thing. And a locker key implies something small, at least portable, and probably valuable."

"But where would Blodgett get a locker key?"

"He'd purchase it just like anyone else. He gets off the train in a strange town. It is dark and he is going to a boardinghouse—not a hotel with a safe, mind you. What more natural than to put the valuable object he is carrying into one of the lockers at the depot?"

I nodded thoughtfully.

"Now we have to rely on our imagination. Why didn't he just pocket the key instead of enclosing it in an envelope and addressing it to himself here at the boardinghouse?" He shrugged his shoulders. "He is a nervous, edgy sort of man. Perhaps just as he finished putting the object away, he noticed someone watching him, or thought he noticed. Just putting the object away in a locker would not do much to ensure its safety if a few minutes after leaving the depot he were waylaid and robbed of the key."

"He could have taken a cab at the station," I objected.

"Monday night? With dozens of strangers coming into town and only one full-time cab available? He probably asked for a cab and was told there was none. Then he in turn was asked where he was going. When he tells them his destination is the Keefe House, he learns, perhaps for the first time, that it is a boardinghouse rather than a hotel. And his informant goes on to tell him that it is only a couple of blocks away and that he can easily walk it.

"All right, I'll grant you that he might have been nervous and thought someone was watching him, but—"

"And I should like to point out," Nicky cut in, "that seeing the envelope addressed to Blodgett in his own hand, and postmarked yesterday from this very town, in conjunction with the feel of the key—all that would set our friend Erik thinking along precisely these lines."

"But hang it all, Nicky, why does it have to be a valuable object? It could be that he had two valises and didn't feel up to carrying both, especially if he was going to walk. What more natural than to put one in a locker and carry the other, the one that contains his shaving kit?"

"He's only going to be here for a couple of days. Two bags are most unlikely. Besides, if it were only a valise that contained a change of underwear and a couple of extra shirts, he would not bother to mail himself the key. He would just pocket it."

"I suppose you are suggesting that it is the Adelphi Bowl that he left in the locker. What did he say it was worth?"

Nicky nodded with relish. "He didn't say, except that it was priceless. Of course, what he had in mind was that it was unique and hence no price could be set on it. But even if it were broken up, I fancy the gold and the gems would come to many thousands of dollars."

"Dammit all, Nicky, a man doesn't go lugging something like that around with him and then leave it in a railroad locker."

"Why not?" Nicky demanded. "If it's small and portable, what better way of transporting it from one place to another than by having someone carry it there? I imagine it has its own fitted carrying case with a handle and looks like an overnight bag. Is it your idea that it should be transported in an armored car with a guard? That *would* be dangerous. It would be alerting every thief in the area. It's natural for you to think that way since your work does not call for handling valuable objects. But those who normally do are a lot more matter-of-fact about it. I knew a diamond merchant who used to travel about a great deal. He carried a fortune in unmounted stones in little folds of paper—parcels he called them—and these he carried in a wallet in his inside breast pocket."

"Then your idea is that Erik sees an envelope addressed by Blodgett to himself—"

"And postmarked from here," Nicky interjected.

"All right, and postmarked from here, and he feels a key inside it and knowing that Blodgett is going to display the Adelphi Bowl, comes to the same conclusion that you have, that it is at present resting in a locker in our modest little depot, instead of in the Bursar's safe at the university, having been previously sent down by the museum authorities."

"Precisely."

"Then why does he bother to steam open the envelope?" I asked triumphantly. "Why doesn't he just tear it open and take out the key and go down to the depot and get it? Or isn't he as sure as you are and intends to examine the contents of the locker first and then if it is not the Bowl, seal the key up in the envelope again?"

"No—no—no," said Nicky testily. "He's sure enough, but he can't just go down there and take it. There's no train out of here at this time for one thing. For another, Blodgett will miss the letter. We know it came in. Suspicion would point— Suspicion?—no, certainty would point to Erik. And how far do you suppose he would get? Look there."

He was standing near the window and I joined him there. On the sidewalk just beneath our windows stood Erik. He stood a moment looking in either direction, and then with his hands thrust deep in his pockets, for there was still a bite to the air, he turned to the right and headed toward the depot at a brisk walk.

Nicky turned away. "No danger," he said. "He will go down to the depot and deposit a quarter in one of the lockers and put that in the envelope. No, he won't. Blodgett might remember the location of his locker. He'll remove the Bowl from Blodgett's locker to another and then put the original key back in the envelope."

"And what do we do about it?" I asked. "Shall I call the police and have them—"

"Call the police?" Nicky stared at me in disbelief. "For what?" he demanded. "Because a young man chooses to boil some water in order to make a cup of instant coffee rather than go to the trouble of preparing a percolator?"

"But going down to the depot—"

"To get a timetable, I imagine,"

It suddenly came to me that I had been had, that Nicky was merely paying me back for my foolish little wager, and that indeed nothing had happened except that Erik had boiled a kettle of water.

Nevertheless, I was uneasy, and the next morning, after Nicky had left, I called my office to tell them that I would not be in that day. I sat near the window where I could command a view of the street. Shortly after ten, I saw Erik leave and head for the university. I put on my topcoat and followed him, keeping about a block behind him, but being careful to keep him in sight all the time. As we approached the university, I quickened my pace and drew nearer to him so as not to lose him in the crowd. I kept him in sight all morning. When he went into a meeting room and took a seat in front, I followed and found a seat in the rear. At noon, I saw him enter the cafeteria and only then did I leave him and head for home. Nicky was in the room when I arrived.

"Didn't you go to your office today?" he asked with a little smirk of amusement on his vinegary face.

"No, I didn't," I said shortly.

I took a seat near the window and stared moodily at the street below while Nicky continued the perusal of his interminable blue books. Presently I saw Erik striding along and a moment later I heard him taking the steps two at a time. He was evidently in high spirits. We could hear him moving around in his room and I assumed he was packing.

A quarter of an hour later he knocked at our door. "I'm so glad you're both in," he said. "I am leaving now. I'm taking the one-thirty out. It was nice meeting you."

"We'll walk you down to the depot," said Nicky. "There'll be quite a few leaving on this train. I ought to say good-bye to some of them."

"And did you profit from the Convocation?" Nicky asked as we walked along.

The young man grinned. "I had one offer of a job," he said, "but it's in India."

Although we were early, there were a number already at the depot waiting for the train. We stood there, engaged in desultory conversation. A number of people whom we had met nodded to us and one or two came over to shake hands and say good-bye. It was while we were thus engaged that Erik drifted away toward the news counter. He purchased a magazine to read on the train and then sauntered on to the bank of lockers just beyond. I was about to follow him when Nicky signaled me to remain where I was. Then *he* followed him.

The train pulled in and the crowd surged forward to get on. I waited, wondering what was happening. Finally the conductor shouted, All Aboard, and it was only then that I saw Erik, running to get aboard the train. I was about to intercept him, when I saw Nicky. He was sauntering and looked smug and self-satisfied.

"Well?" I demanded.

For answer Nicky held out his hand and there was a locker key on his upraised palm.

"What did he say?"

"I asked him for the key and he saw that I knew," said Nicky. "He asked me if someone had seen him, and I said, 'No, but I heard you boiling up some water.' Then he gave me the key."

"Now what?" I asked.

"I think as County Attorney you ought to have enough influence with the station master or whoever is in charge here to open Locker 518 so that we can transfer the Bowl back to it." He sounded testy.

As we walked back to the boardinghouse I said, "Do you think we were right in letting him go, Nicky? After all, we are compounding a felony."

"Would it have been better if it had all been made public and the university involved in a scandal, not to mention that Blodgett would have lost his job?"

I did not press the matter.

When we got back to the boardinghouse, Blodgett was

there. "I guess I missed Erik," he said. "I planned to get back in time to see him off, but there were some last-minute arrangements that I had to make for my paper tonight."

"Has the Bowl arrived yet?" asked Nicky gravely.

"Arrived? Why, I brought it with me. I checked it in one of the lockers at the railroad station."

"At the railroad station?"

Blodgett laughed. "It's quite safe, I assure you. By far the best place. I'll pick it up on my way and then cab over to the university. Will you be coming to the meeting tonight?"

"We have an engagement," said Nicky, "but we'll try to get in if only for a few minutes."

We did not go to the meeting. Instead, we spent the evening playing chess at the Faculty Club. By this time the visitors had all gone and the place was quiet and peaceful. At nine o'clock Professor Richardson came in. There had been photographs and he was carrying his academic gown and hood in the crook of his arm. He sat down heavily and fanned himself with his mortarboard.

"Thank God, that's over," he said.

"Successful Convocation, Professor?" I asked.

"All right, I guess, as these things go," he said. "Of course, Prex would have liked a little more publicity than we got. I gather he would have liked something really dramatic to make headlines, a murder perhaps, or the theft of the university uranium supply."

"You should have told us earlier," said Nicky. "We might have arranged it."

The Bread and Butter Case

ON Wednesday nights when I dine at the Faculty Club I am there as Nicky Welt's guest, presumably to balance the Friday nights that he comes to my house for an evening of chess.

When Ellis Johnston, County Attorney for Suffolk, dropped in on me late one Wednesday afternoon in January on a matter of business, I invited him to join us for dinner. Frankly, I was not certain how Nicky would take my presumption in burdening him with another guest—Nicky can be quite sensitive about such things—but it went off very well. He remembered having met Johnston at my house and was pleased to see him again. He shepherded us into the dining room like an indulgent uncle taking a couple of favorite nephews out of school for a treat. He sat us on either side of him and urged the richest dishes on us when the waiter came to take our orders.

We talked about the weather of course. Our winter that year was setting meteorological records. We had had three major snowstorms during the month of December unrelieved by any perceptible thaw. The pattern had continued into January with a ten-inch snowstorm on New Year's Day, a blizzard three days later that had left sixteen inches of snow, and a cold spell which had kept the thermometer around zero for a fortnight. And when at the end of that period the temperature did go up somewhat, it was only to deposit more snow.

Johnston said, "Driving through the streets of the city is like running a bobsled course. The snowbanks on either side of you are so high, you can't see the people on the sidwalks. Why only yesterday we found a man buried in the snowbank. It was on Holgate Street. That's not a main traffic artery to be sure, but it's a fairly well-traveled street. He had been there since the big blizzard on the fourth. That's three weeks. Imagine the hundreds of people who walked past him in that time and no one the wiser."

"I heard the item on the news broadcast last night," I said. "There is a suspicion of murder, isn't there?"

"No suspicion," said Johnston grimly. "It's definitely murder. His head was bashed in and he had been laid out with his hands by his sides as neatly as you please. It's hardly the way a man would fall accidentally."

"It sounds as though it might be interesting," I said.

Johnston shrugged. "Just another bread and butter case."

"And what is a bread and butter case?" asked Nicky.

Johnston laughed shortly. "My brother-in-law has a hardware store," he said irrelevantly, "and any time you go in there you are apt to see a woman buying a frying pan or a man buying a garden hose. Now, even if they are regular customers of his, he still may not see them again for a couple of months. So he regards those sales as jam. In a sense, they're almost accidental. But the carpenters, plumbers, and electricians who trade with him—they're his bread and butter. He can count on seeing them several times a week right through the year. Now in the city we have a sizable population of professional criminals. We can depend on them to give us work week in and week out. So they're our bread and butter."

"And is your procedure any different in bread and butter cases?" asked Nicky.

"Well, we usually know who is responsible for a particular job almost as soon as it's done, by the way it's done, or by way of rumor through the grapevine, but mostly because we make it a point to know these people. We know how they think and how they feel. We know what pressures are at work and what balance of forces obtain at any particular time. By the same token, these people being professional are adept at covering their tracks. So we are usually in the position of knowing who committed a particular crime, but we have no proof. Your kind of reasoning and analysis would be useless in these cases, Professor. You'd have no clues to start with. Frankly, there's nothing subtle about our methods in bread and butter cases. We don't knock them around, although quite a bit of it was done under my predecessor a few years back. We question those involved—at length. You see, we're looking for a chink in their armor, so we can get a wedge into it and open them up. We may have to put pressure on one person in order to get him to put pressure in turn on another who may have given the suspect an alibi. Once the alibi is broken, we have our case. Take this present business for example. When the police lieutenant notified me that John Reilly had got his lumps, I suggested immediately that he pick up Tommy Jordan for questioning, and he grinned at me and told me that they already had.

"Strictly speaking, John Reilly was not of the underworld. At least we were never able to pin anything on him. He was on the fringe, you might say. He owned some slum tenement houses and a bunch of sleazy boarding-houses, and he did some bail-bonding and some money lending. A bachelor, about fifty, he was a little jockey of a man, always dressed to the nines, with an exaggerated sense of personal dignity. If you called him John or Reilly, he'd correct you. 'It's *Mister,*' he would say. So he was known around as Mister John.

"He had a little box of an office in the Lawyers' Building right in Courthouse Square. He was never there, but you could leave a message for him with his clerk, Cyrus Gerber, and it would reach him. That was where the people who owed him money left it, and the janitors of his properties left the rents they collected. As I said, we make it our business to know about these people, and we knew that Terry Jordan had it in for Mister John.

"Terry Jordan is a big broth of a lad, goodhearted, but not overly endowed with brains. He graduated from juvenile delinquency to small-time crime, but was never very successful at it. He is what is known in his circle as a born patsy—you know, always the last one over the fence. He finally got a job as assistant manager, which is polite for bouncer, at the Hi-Hat Café. There was a waitress there, a big blond amazon of a girl, called Lily Cherry. He's a good-looking boy, so it's not surprising that after a while she became his girl."

"You mean, they became engaged?" asked Nicky.

Johnston smiled at him affectionately. "No, Professor, they didn't become engaged, and neither did they get married when he moved into her apartment. It was just a convenient arrangement and they both continued to work at the Hi-Hat. Then Terry got restless again. We picked him up on a burglary charge and he got a year in the pen. There was no question about his guilt, you understand, and it was only his own stupidity that enabled us to pin it on him, but somehow, perhaps from something the police detective said, he got it into his head that Mister John had had something to do with his arrest. There was nothing to it—just an overzealous policeman hoping to get a lead. It happens all the time. It's hard to imagine even a light-brain like Terry Jordan taking it seriously."

"Unless he wanted to believe it," Nicky suggested.

Johnston favored him with a quick appreciative glance. "You mean so he could tell himself that it wasn't his fault. You've got a point there, Professor. Anyway, there it was. Whether justified or not, Terry thought Mister John had fingered him, and it was known that he thought so. Now, for a supposedly smart man, Mister John did a foolish thing. Although he knew how Terry felt, nevertheless he began to make up to Lily and in a little while he took Terry's place in the apartment. From the girl's point of view it was a pretty good deal: it enabled her to stop working; she got some new pretties; and she even had Mister John's convertible to ride around in.

"Now Terry didn't expect her to sit home and twiddle her thumbs waiting for him to get out of jail. He wasn't married to her and there was probably nothing very intense between them. But this combination of the two things—his original feeling about Mister John and now his taking over his girl—"

"King David and Bathsheba," Nicky murmured.

"That's it exactly," said Johnston. "And it was also a matter of prestige. Everybody knew that he blamed Mister John for his arrest. So this was adding insult to injury. He had to avenge his honor, as it were, or he would be the laughingstock of his circle. At that, I didn't expect murder, although I would have been surprised if he didn't knock him about a bit. Maybe that's all he planned to do, but just struck a little harder than he intended.

"Terry got out on the second of January. He went to see Lily. We know that. Then he began making inquiries around after Mister John. He even went to his office and asked Cyrus Gerber where he could find him. I told you he was not too bright."

Johnston leaned forward and ticked off the points on his fingers. "What do we have? We know that Terry had a grudge against Mister John—that's motive. He gets out of prison on the second and he starts looking for him—that's opportunity. Weapon? Any blunt instrument, a wrench, a stick, will do. Now as to method: the fourth, that's just two days later, we have a blizzard;

he locates Mister John; he steals a car—he's rather gifted that way, but as a matter of fact, in this weather we've been having, lots of folks don't turn their motors off when they stop for a while. So he steals a car and he catches up with Mister John. Maybe he hits him over the head with a wrench to persuade him to get into the car, but he hits a little too hard and the man is dead. It's around four o'clock and we're having a blizzard. There were very few cars on the road and almost no pedestrians. In that driving snow visibility was about fifty feet.

"He drives along looking for a place to park the body. There's about six inches of newly fallen snow at the time and both sides of the streets are lined with snowbanks maybe four feet high from the previous snows. He finds a likely spot and pulls over to the side of the road. No one coming toward him and in the rearview mirror he sees no one coming behind him. He opens the door of the car, picks up the body and lays it on the snowbank. He pushes some snow on top of it. He knows there'll be another six to ten inches before the storm subsides and then the plows will come along. He's perfectly safe. No one is going to stop in that kind of weather to see if he is in trouble and needing help. If you were out driving, you kept on going, hoping you wouldn't get stuck yourself.

"In a few minutes, he's back in the car and drives off—"

"What makes you so sure of the time and date?" I asked.

Johnston grinned. "We're sure all right. It wasn't too hard. We cut cores out of the snowbank around the body and then analyzed it the way a geologist would. You see we knew just when it snowed and how much. The

Street Department has records of when they plowed and when they sanded. The combination of the two gave us a pretty accurate record."

"And what does Terry say?" I asked.

"Oh, he denies everything, of course."

"Did you tell him that you know that he had been looking for Mister John?"

"He insists he never got to see him. He maintains that when he went to see Lily, she told him that she and Mister John were going to get married. They were going to drive down to Florida and get married on the way. And he insists that he was looking for Mister John merely to tell him that he bore him no grudge and to wish him luck."

"Quite possible," Nicky murmured.

Johnston gave him a wry smile. "You joking, Professor? Why would Mister John want to marry Lily, especially when he had been living with her for a year. I'll admit she might think so, though. She's not overbright either. In any case, she backs up Terry's story."

"Did she report him missing?" I asked.

Johnston shook his head. "No one reported him missing."

"Isn't that in itself suspicious?" I asked. "If he was her fiancé and was missing for three weeks—"

"At first sight it would appear so," said Johnston, "but in all fairness, it doesn't mean too much. Those people wouldn't be likely to go to the police. For all she knew, his absence might merely mean that he had some deal going out of town. Actually, there is no one who would be likely to report his absence. The man was a bachelor. Except for a widowed sister-in-law and her son, he has no family at all. Who else would miss him? The clerk? He said he didn't see Mister John for a couple of weeks at a time even when he was right around Courthouse Square every day. He knew nothing about the business because that's the way Mister John wanted it. If someone came in to pay money, he took it and gave a receipt. If someone wanted to get in touch with Mister John, he left him a note. He got paid by the month, so he wouldn't even start thinking about it for another week. Of course, after a while, say a couple of months, his friends or Lily or the clerk might begin inquiring around to see what they could learn by the grapevine. Then, if they heard nothing, they might risk going to the police. But that would be after months of absence. That leaves his sister-in-law and her son, Frank Reilly. They're respectable people who have as little to do with him as possible. She is a retired schoolteacher. Frank, her son, is about thirty and unmarried and lives with her. He runs a card and record shop not far from where they live in the suburbs. Normally, they wouldn't hear from Mister John for months at a time. The last time they saw him was early in November. Frank had a chance to buy the store he was working in. His boss had to go to Arizona for his health and there was a chance to get it at a bargain price. Frank went to see his uncle, much against his mother's will, I gather, and Mister John gave him the money, six thousand dollars.

"In going over Mister John's books yesterday that checked out. For obvious reasons, Mister John didn't go in much for keeping records. He didn't even keep his old bank statements. Most of his business, I imagine, was done in cash, but he did pay some things by check and there was a three-tier checkbook in his desk. The stubs showed that three checks for two thousand dollars each had been made out to Frank Reilly on November seventh."

"Three checks?"

"According to Frank, that was so that he could dicker. He was to offer two thousand first and then four thousand if that didn't work, and finally the six if it was absolutely necessary. I gather that Frank, who is a kind of arty young man, a little on the swish side to tell the truth, thought it undignified to haggle and didn't try to. Obviously, he is not one of the great financial brains of our time, but he seems like a decent sort and he's devoted to his mother who is crippled with arthritis and hobbles about on a cane. The big advantage of the store from his point of view was that it was located not far from his house and he could run over whenever his mother needed him. They're really very nice people."

We had finished our dinner and at Nicky's suggestion we adjourned to the Commons Room for our coffee. The waiter moved a coffee table in front of the fireplace and set armchairs around it. When he had served us and we were once more alone, I said flatly, "I don't see that you have much of a case."

"We don't," Johnston admitted, "not yet, but we have the man."

"But you can't keep him," I insisted.

"We can hold him for questioning. And we'll question him all right. We'll take him over every minute of his life since he got out of jail. We'll question him again and again. And if he contradicts himself just once, that will give us our wedge."

"You could probably get me to confess under the same treatment," I said.

Johnston flushed. He was on the point of replying in anger, but he managed to control himself. "We fight fire with fire," he said stiffly. "We know he killed him—"

"I can see why you think he killed him," Nicky interrupted, "but I can't understand why he buried him."

Johnston turned to Nicky, very pointedly, as if to ignore me. "Naturally he wouldn't want the body found. He did it for the same reason that a murderer buries his victim in the woods or ties a weight around him and dumps him over a bridge into the ocean."

Nicky shook his head. "Surely, Mr. Johnston, you see a difference between burying a man in a snowbank along a busy street on the one hand and burying him in the woods or dumping him into the ocean on the other."

"What's the difference?" Johnston demanded.

Nicky ventured a wry smile. "In the latter case, the action is accompanied by the hope, not unjustified, that the body will never be found at all, or if found, then found in an unrecognizable condition. But in burying a man in a snowbank along one of the streets of a city, there is a certainty that he will be found and readily recognized and identified when found. He will have been preserved in deep freeze as it were. On the basis of our normal weather the discovery would be delayed by a few days or a week. Even with the extraordinary winter we have been having, the murderer could only hope for a delay of a month or so."

"Well, it would give him that much more time for a getaway," said Johnston.

Nicky shook his head decisively. "With modern means of transportation one doesn't need weeks or even days to make a getaway. A headstart of an hour or two, enough time to get to the railroad or bus station or to the air terminal, is sufficient. Besides, Terry didn't try to get away, did he? Your police had no difficulty in picking him up, did they? What I want to know is why the murderer didn't just open the door of the car and push the body of his victim out and then ride on. The body would have fallen at the foot of the snowbank and even if discovered almost immediately, there would be a good chance that it would be assumed that he was the victim of a hit and run driver. If the body were wholly or partly covered by the falling snow, there would be a good chance that the body *would* be hit by a passing motorist, or even by the snowplow. In either case, the resultant contusions would serve to disguise the blow on the head, and the murder could pass as an accident."

"He might have panicked," Johnston suggested.

"Then he would have been even more likely to have dumped the body and run," Nicky retorted. "I'm afraid you don't understand the full implication of my question. The effect of burying the body in the snowbank was to delay its discovery for a few days. Since it is such an unusual action, it is fair to assume that this is precisely what the murderer wanted."

"What could he hope to gain by that?" Johnston demanded.

Nicky pursed his lips as though he had bitten into a sour lemon. "I'm sure there are any number of possibilities, but one that suggests itself to me immediately is that if he had a dated check of Mister John's, he might hope to cash it."

Johnston raised an appreciative eyebrow. "You mean if he were known to be dead, the bank would automatically stop payment on any check dated after the date of his death. It's an interesting possibility, Professor. It could be that Terry didn't intend to kill Mister John or even to beat him up, only to shake him down for a large sum of money. That might explain why he wasn't afraid to make open inquiry for him. All right, he braces Mister John for a stake. But he's not taking fifty or a hundred dollars. He demands a thousand or two maybe. 'I don't carry that kind of money around,' says Mister John. 'I'll tell you what—I'll give you a check.' So he writes out a check but he dates it ahead a few days accidentally on purpose, planning to stop payment on it. That's the sort of thing I can imagine Mister John doing. But it doesn't work. Terry spots the mistake and in his anger he wallops him over the head. But he hits too hard, so now he has a body on his hands. If he can keep the death secret for a few days, however, he might still be able to get the money. So he drives along—" Quite suddenly, the eagerness went out of his voice. "It won't do, Professor. Terry would realize that to cash the check would tie him to the murder. He may be dumb, but he's not that dumb."

An idle thought had been pecking at my mind and now the pieces were falling into place. I had been trying to visualize the principals in the affair and my attention had been focused on the tall, blond person of Lily Cherry. "Look here, Nicky, I think I see what you're driving at. You're taking this business of Mister John's wanting to marry Lily at face value."

Nicky's nod of encouragement urged me on. "Here's a big amazon of a woman, and Mister John is a little shrimp of a man. Her handsome lover comes out of jail and is now available. Naturally she prefers him to Mister John.

Well, she's big enough to handle Mister John. She doesn't have to go looking for him—he's at her apartment. She has a car—his. They were planning to go to Florida and get married. Naturally, she'd need clothes and she'd put it up to Mister John. So he would sit down and write her a nice big check."

Nicky smiled. "And why would he give her a dated check?"

Several possible reasons suggested themselves to me, but before I could offer them, Johnston growled. "Theories, just a bunch of fine theories that don't mean anything. Now I can settle this dated check business right now. We went through Mister John's books with a fine-tooth comb. There wasn't much to go through, so we couldn't have overlooked anything. There were no checks missing from his checkbook. Every check that had been issued had a stub properly made out."

"Have you received this month's statement of his account from the bank yet?" Nicky asked.

"We asked them for it, and they promised to prepare it right away. I imagine it's on my desk this minute."

"Then I am prepared to make a wager," said Nicky. He drew an old-fashioned coin purse from his trouser pocket. Unsnapping the catch, he poked around in its depths with a lean forefinger. Then with a faint sigh, he drew out a quarter and placed it primly on the coffee table in front of him.

Johnston smiled. He tossed a quarter onto the table so that it landed beside Nicky's coin. "All right, Professor, you're faded. What's your bet?"

"I am prepared to wager that in the bank statement that you think is now resting on your desk, you will find a check for two thousand dollars made out to Frank Reilly."

"Frank Reilly, the nephew? You mean that he did manage to get the business for four thousand dollars and kept two thousand for himself?"

"I mean that the story of three checks being made out so that he could dicker with the owner of the store is all poppycock."

"What's wrong with it?" asked Johnston.

"It's not the way you dicker. The spread is too great. If the asking price is six thousand dollars, you might start with four and then compromise on five or five thousand five hundred. But you wouldn't arrange to go from four to six in one jump. Frank, not being much of a businessman, might not realize it, but Mister John certainly would. Besides, I don't think Mister John would just hand over six thousand dollars to the likes of Frank and tell him to go ahead and buy a business."

"What's the matter with Frank?" asked Johnston.

"He's thirty and unmarried and has no trade or profession. And since his mother was a schoolteacher it was probably not for lack of opportunity or because of parental opposition. He is what we used to call a mama's boy. He has probably had a succession of small jobs ending up with that of clerk in a small neighborhood record shop. My guess is that Mister John looked over the business very carefully, saw that it was a good buy, and then arranged for Frank to make payment in three equal monthly payments. So he made out the three checks and dated them—"

"But the stubs all show the same date," Johnston objected.

"The stubs, yes, because he probably made them out first and all at once. But in making out the checks, he would naturally date them as he wanted them paid, one for November, one for December, and the last for January. The chances are that he couldn't release six thousand dollars all at once, anyway. That's a sizable sum. Now that last check was dated January seventh, and it was very important that the bank should have no reason to suspect that Mister John was anything but alive on that day."

"Are you trying to say that it was his nephew who killed him?"

"I am saying that Frank buried him in the snowbank. I don't think he'd have the nerve to kill him. I suspect that it was his mother, that dear old schoolteacher, who killed him, probably with that same stick that she hobbles around on."

"But why?" asked Johnston. "Why?"

"Because he was going to get married, of course. He came out to tell them. Look here, don't you see the essential falsity of the picture they succeeded in palming off on you. And if false, then it suggests guilt. Mister John probably did visit them only a couple of times a year, but it was not because they discouraged his visits. He had an exaggerated sense of personal dignity, you said. If they had once indicated that he was unwelcome, he probably would never have come again. Why would he want to visit them? What was there in that ménage that would attract a man like Mister John? The only reason he visited them at all, and that as little as possible, was because they were his only living relatives. Those were duty calls he made. I'm sure Frank saw him more often, however. Living on a schoolteacher's pension and a clerk's wages, they must have needed help every now and then, fifty or a hundred dollars that Mister John would give him in cash. It stands to reason that Frank would not have approached him for six thousand if he had not received smaller sums in the past. The old lady might have thought that the sun rises and sets on her precious boy, but she was under no illusion about his capacity to make a living. What would happen to him after she died and her pension would stop? Well, there was always Uncle John to help the boy out. But now, at the age of fifty, he was planning to marry. That meant that even while he lived, the money would not be forthcoming so readily. And in the event of his death, instead of the money going to Frank, it would go to the widow. So she struck with her cane. And then she had her son carry the body to the car in the garage. That precious pair, with the body of Mister John making a grisly third, probably drove out with the intention of dropping it on the side of the road—until they bethought themselves of the final payment that had to be made on the store."

Johnston stared at Nicky, speechless for the moment. Then he jumped up. "There's bound to be somebody still in the office. I'm going to phone and check that bank statement."

"There's a phone booth in the hall outside," I offered.

While Johnston was gone, we waited, Nicky and I, in silence. There were questions that I wanted to ask, but somehow it did not seem fair while Johnston was gone. Nicky seemed perfectly at ease, but I noticed that his fingers were drumming a steady tattoo on the arm of his chair.

In a few minutes, Johnston returned. "Pick up the marbles, Professor," he said sourly. "The check was there all right."

I could not resist a sly dig. "Then you mean, Nicky," I asked innocently, "that Terry had absolutely nothing to do with it?"

But Nicky turned on me sharply. "He had everything to do with it."

"What did he do?" Johnston and I asked in unison.

"He got out of jail, that's what he did. That triggered off the whole thing. I imagine that Mister John was very much in love with the girl. He must have been to take the risk he did. I think they were happy together. I think that between the two, Terry and Mister John, Lily would probably have chosen the older man anyway. But Mister John could not know that. All that he could think of was that this handsome young man was back on the scene and that Lily might go back to him. So he asked her to marry him as a means of tying her to him. And when she told Terry, he probably realized that it was a fine opportunity for her. Being an intrinsically decent young man, he wished her luck and assured her that he had no hard feelings. And then he tried to see Mister John to assure him that he had nothing to fear from him."

"Like the hero in a soap opera or a TV western," Johnston sneered.

"Precisely," said Nicky. "People like Terry get their ideas of morality and ethics, as do the rest of us, from the books they read and the plays they see." He could not forbear to add with a frosty little smile, "You have to realize that, Mr. Johnston, in order to understand them."

The Man on the Ladder

IN the parlance of the undergraduate, Gentleman Johnny—more respectfully Professor John Baxter Bowman, Chairman of the History Department—was a swinger, with a taste and interest in clothes not usually associated with the professoriat. Though he lived at Mrs. Hanrahan's, a roominghouse occupied largely by impecunious graduate students, his dress for that staid New England community was flamboyant to the point of eccentricity. He wore a fitted overcoat with an astrakhan collar, lemon yellow gloves, and was the only man in the university, perhaps in town, with a derby. For one who had been so long at the university, surprisingly little was known about his personal life other than that he had been divorced years ago and had a son he never talked about.

There was nothing eccentric about Johnny Bowman's scholarship, however. His reputation was solidly based on countless papers and three bound books published by the university press. Then quite suddenly he acquired fame far beyond the limits of our town or the parochial world of scholars. His latest book, *Growth of the Cities,* won the Gardner Prize for Historical Literature which carried a cash award of five hundred dollars. But what mattered far more was that, because of the prize, the critics took another look at the book, or rather looked at it for the first time since none of the leading reviewers had bothered with it when it first appeared, and discovered that it was "a work of solid scholarship"; "a major contribution to the field"; and that he was "in the tradition of the great philosopher-historians." Overnight the book began to sell, within a month another printing was necessary, and it even appeared one week on the best-seller lists. It goes without saying that at faculty parties, sooner or later the conversation got around to Johnny Bowman's fabulous luck and to envious speculation on the size of his royalties.

I myself barely knew the man. He was rarely at the Faculty Club, and faculty wives had given up inviting him to parties long before I came to the university. And then I left the Law Faculty to run for County Attorney, so I saw even less of him.

Since the President had suggested I take an extended leave of absence instead of resigning, I was still officially a member of the faculty and as such was invited to the President's annual Christmas reception for the faculty. I accepted not only because of past favors from Prex but because I assumed Professor Bowman would be there and I had a not unnatural desire to renew my acquaintance with a celebrity.

Traditionally, the President's Christmas reception is held on the first day of vacation. Years ago when travel was less convenient and more expensive, most of the faculty spent the vacation in town. But nowadays faculty and student body alike flee the campus the moment the last class is over, so only a small group turns up. Nevertheless it is still held on the first day of vacation, rather than a day or two earlier when more might be able to attend. Tradition dies hard in New England.

I walked over to the reception with my good friend Professor Nicholas Welt. He was planning to catch the night train to Chicago where he would spend the vacation; but as the incumbent of the Snowdon Professorship of English Literature, the oldest and perhaps the most prestigious chair in the college, he felt he should put in an appearance.

We were greeted by Prex and his wife, dutifully nibbled the spreads and sampled the punch. Finding the last wanting, we began working our way to the door when we were hailed by Jan Ladlo. He entered with his new bride of a few weeks in tow. He introduced me; Nicky already knew her—she was a graduate student and had taken courses with him.

"And how does it feel to be Mrs. Ladlo instead of Mrs. Johnson?" he asked.

"Just fine," she said and put her hand under her husband's arm.

Jan Ladlo is a short, pudgy man with a round balding head, a bulbous nose and protruding myopic eyes. Nevertheless, as an associate professor in the History Department who was still on the right side of forty, he had been considered one of our most eligible bachelors by the faculty wives who are always on the lookout for their spinster sorority sisters.

"Have you been here long, Professor?" Ladlo asked Nicky and inquired if Johnny Bowman had shown up.

"Apparently not," said Nicky. "I guess you will have to represent the department."

I realized that only the older men presumed to call Nicky by his first name, the rest invariably addressed him by title. Not that Nicky is himself old. He is only two or three years older than I, in fact, but he has prematurely white hair—my own is just beginning to gray at the temples—and his gnomelike face is lined. But that's not it either—Bowman, who is several years older than Nicky, is called Johnny by the youngest instructors. I suppose it's Nicky's general manner, the way he listens to you as he might to some luckless freshman asking for an extension on a term paper, that makes you feel young and callow in his presence.

"Oh, he'll probably be along later," said Ladlo. "And Bob Dykes said he was coming, so I guess the History Department will make a pretty good showing before the evening is over."

"I heard Johnny was planning to give up teaching," I said, "now that he can live on his royalties."

Ladlo laughed. "He'll never give up teaching. As a matter of fact, his royalties on *Growth of the Cities* won't come to very much—certainly not enough to retire on. It's the next book he expects will make him some money, big money. He's known now and the reviewers will be watching for it."

"How soon before it comes out?"

Ladlo shrugged his shoulders. "You know how secretive Bowman is. Bob Dykes has been helping him on it. He thinks it's still a long way off. Oh, there's Bob now." He waved and called him over. "Where's Laura? Isn't she coming?"

"Oh, she's off to Florida to visit her folks," Dykes said.

"She went alone?" asked Mrs. Ladlo, unable to understand how a wife could leave her husband for even a few days.

"I'm going to try to join her," said Dykes with a grin. "There was some work I was doing for Bowman, and I felt I ought to stay until I finished it."

Dykes is an assistant professor in the department, and although not yet thirty, is regarded as a comer. He is a handsome young man, tall and slim, with an aquiline profile and deep-set eyes. His mop of black hair is curiously bisected by a single lock of white which adds a somewhat romantic touch. Everyone liked Dykes. There was something of the small boy about him that disarmed criticism. He was a gadgeteer and a hobbyist with great enthusiasm for anything he happened to be engaged in at the moment—whether it was ham radio, or photography, or rock hunting. As he talked of them, their potentials would expand until you found yourself believing that his interest in ham radio was not just a love of gadgetry but a desire to expand his horizon through enlarged communication; and that his rock collection satisfied not merely an itch for ownership, but gave him a greater understanding of Mother Earth. And yet his interests also had a curious boyish practicality—he had sold some of his rock specimens to museums and even to our own geology department, and as for his camera, he claimed it had helped pay his way through graduate school.

"We were talking about Bowman's new book," I said. "Is it almost finished?"

Dykes smiled. "It could take another year. You know how these things are. I'm planning to spend the vacation working on it full time."

"Not on the house?" asked Ladlo with a twinkle. Everyone twitted Dykes about his latest hobby—his new house. It was an old Victorian ark of a place that he had bought last year, and he never tired of regaling us at the Faculty Club with the wonders of the place—"built to last; not like the shoddy cracker boxes they're putting up nowadays." It was spacious and there was room to move around. And he had answers to all objections. It would cost a fortune to heat? He would seal off all rooms not in use. Repairs? He could do most of them himself and enjoy it. He might even consider cutting up the house into small apartments as his neighbor who had bought its twin across the street was planning to do.

"Well, there are a couple of small jobs around the house I may get around to, as relaxation from Bowman's work," he admitted with a smile. "Anyone seen him tonight?"

"Just coming in now," said Ladlo nodding toward the door.

Bowman had a young man with him, a blond good-looking youngster in his twenties, and he steered him in our direction. "I'd like you all to meet my son Charles," he said somewhat diffidently. "Charles is with a publishing house, an editor. He'll be staying for a week or so and he's offered to take a look at the manuscript." He turned to Dykes. "Isn't that splendid, Bobby?"

Dykes nodded slowly and then grinned. "We can sure use all the help we can get."

Nicky glanced at his watch. "If I'm going to catch my train, I'd better get started. It's a longish walk to the station."

"Taking the eight o'clock?" asked Dykes. "I've got my car here. I'll drive you over."

"Very kind of you," said Nicky.

As we started for the door Bowman asked Dykes if he were coming back. "I don't think so. I left Duke in the car and I ought to take him home." Bowman asked if he'd be around the next day, and Dykes said he thought he would. "Good, we might drop in on you," said Bowman.

"Lots been happening in your department," I remarked, as we went outside. "Bowman getting a best-seller, Ladlo getting married—"

"And she's a nice girl, too," Dykes interjected quickly.

"Appears to be."

"Some of the wives of my colleagues haven't been overkind."

"Oh?"

"You know how it is here. They were seen together while she was still a married woman. She was getting a divorce, of course, but they didn't know that. And then when the divorce came through and they got married, there were some that thought she ought not remarry right away, as though she had just been widowed."

We neared the car and a dog began to bark vehemently. Dykes smiled. "Good old Duke. He knows my step."

He had acquired the dog shortly after moving into the new house; ostensibly, to provide protection and companionship for Laura when she was alone. But it was obvious to anyone who knew Dykes that he had bought Duke because, like any boy, he wanted a dog. He had spent hours training him—the usual tricks: to heel, to come on call—and for the last, he had acquired one of those silent whistles which he wore on a cord around his neck. Duke was no ordinary dog. He was a briard, a Belgian sheepdog, a huge creature with a long rough iron-gray coat, the shaggy fur covering even his face so that you wondered how he could see. I remember when someone observed it must cost a small fortune to feed the beast, Dykes replied that although the dog did eat a lot he was thinking of getting a female and breeding her and selling the puppies. It struck me as a perfect Dykesian solution.

Without question the dog was well trained. After expressing its obvious joy at seeing his master, he sat sedately besides Dykes in the front seat and Nicky and I got in back. As we drove, much to Nicky's annoyance—he is always nervous in cars—Dykes kept turning around to give us examples of the dog's intelligence, and we were relieved to arrive at the station without mishap.

We saw Nicky off and then Dykes asked if I'd like to stop for a minute and see his place. But I begged off.

"Some other time. I really want to get home now."

"Okay, some other time it is." He seemed hurt at my refusal.

We drove in silence until we reached my door. I thanked him for the lift and remarked it seemed a shame he had to stay in town during vacation, what with his wife away and all. "Is the book so far along that these few days will make a difference?"

He shook his head. "We're a long way from finishing, but Johnny was insistent. Maybe he's right, because he's got plenty of trouble on this one."

The next day whatever trouble Johnny Bowman might

have had with the book was over. In fact, all his troubles were over. Johnny Bowman was dead.

His death seemingly was the result of idle curiosity. The university was excavating the foundation of a new dormitory. At the crest of High Street where the excavation comes to within a few feet of the roadbed, the police had set out a roadblock and lanterns. Bowman must have gone to peer over the edge to see how the work was progressing. We had our first snowfall of the winter that morning, and although it was light, less than an inch, the ground was slick. The drop at that point was a good thirty feet, and either he had slipped, or the ground at the edge had given way and he had fallen to his death.

Since it was Saturday, there was no one working on the site, and for that matter with vacation, no one was around. A college town becomes a ghost town during the Christmas vacation. The workman who filled and lit the lanterns found him crumpled at the foot of the drop, his derby a few yards away. The body showed the expected contusions, and the medical examiner gave it as his opinion that he had died within minutes of striking the bottom.

Of course the police held an investigation since the death was not due to natural causes. And as D.A., and because of my connection with the university, I felt I ought to take part.

I questioned Mrs. Hanrahan, Bowman's landlady, but learned only that he had slept late that morning and would not have left until sometime around noon.

He stopped at the history office. Professor Ladlo was there, but he had little to offer.

"I must have been the last person to see him alive," he

remarked. "Johnny came in around half past twelve, and we chatted for a few minutes. Then he left saying that he was going to drop in on Bob Dykes, but I've seen Dykes and he said he had been in Norton all day Saturday."

"Had he expected to find Dykes here at the history office? Is that why he came?"

Ladlo shook his head. "I don't think so. When they work together, it's mostly at Dykes' house. No, I guess he came here as a matter of habit as much as anything. He gets his mail here for one thing. Besides, if he were going to Dykes' place, this is on the way."

I questioned Dykes, who confirmed he had not seen Bowman. "I didn't really have an appointment with him," he said. "You heard him. I said I'd be home and he said he might drop around. It was that kind of thing, nothing definite. We've been working here because there's plenty of space and we're not likely to be interrupted, and I have the manuscript and all the notes. Normally, I would have hung around all day. Lord knows I've got plenty to do here. But with Laura gone, I felt kind of restless and I decided to go into Norton to do some last-minute shopping. I left here around eleven and when I got to Norton, I just wandered around the stores. I had a bite and then decided to really make a day of it and I went to a movie—right in the middle of the day," he added wonderingly. "First time I've ever done that sort of thing—go to a movie in the daytime, I mean. And just think, the first time I do something out of the ordinary it results in the death of Johnny Bowman."

"How so?"

"Well, it stands to reason if I had been at home, we

would have worked on the book and I would have driven him home."

"How do you know he ever got to your house?"

"Well of course I don't. I just assumed it. Do you have any evidence . . ." He looked at me questioningly.

I shook my head, but because he was evidently distressed and I wanted to relieve his mind, I said, "It's just more likely that it happened on the way to your house rather than on the way back. The slope to the top of High Street from the history office is a good climb, and I myself usually stop a minute to rest before I go on. I'm just guessing, of course, but I think that when Johnny got to the top of the hill, he stopped, and then quite naturally he walked over to see how the excavation was coming."

I could see that he was grateful for my theory. He nodded his head slowly and thoughtfully. "As a matter of fact, I do the same sort of thing. I don't feel winded when I get to the top—" He grinned at me. "I guess I'm in a little better condition, but I always stop to look at the view. You can see over the whole valley, and I can even see the roof of my house from there."

My visit to the son was more in the nature of a condolence call. But he seemed to take his father's death rather lightly, and I was shocked. I could not refrain from remarking on it.

"What do you expect?" he demanded bitterly. "I knew him about as well as I know you. Since I was thirteen when my parents were divorced, and that's twelve years ago, I've seen my father maybe half a dozen times. I'd get a letter three or four times a year, and that was all."

"Sometimes," I suggested, "it's not easy for the parent

who doesn't get custody to see the children. He may feel that they are resentful and he is hurting them more by seeing them than by staying away."

"He had visiting rights. He never exercised them."

"Then what brought you down at this time? A sudden burst of filial affection?"

"Business. My boss found out that my father had no contract yet for the new book and suggested maybe I could get it for the firm. I thought it might do me some good with them, so I came down."

"Did you tell your father that was why you wanted to see him?"

He had the grace to blush. "No, I just wrote him that I had a week's vacation and would like to see him if he were free."

"And did you get the book for the firm?"

"I didn't broach the subject. I thought I'd play it cool. I just said I'd like to see what he was working on and maybe I could give him some editorial assistance."

I asked if he had seen the manuscript, but he shook his head.

"He said he would see me in the afternoon. We were to have dinner together. I assumed he was planning to bring it with him. I waited around all day, and when he didn't show I called his roominghouse. They said he had left around noon and hadn't returned. I assumed he had forgotten about me. I guess I was annoyed. It was in keeping with the way he had treated me all my life. So I left the hotel and walked around town until I got hungry and—oh yes, I called the hotel once to see if there was a message, and of course there wasn't. So I ate at a restaurant alone. Then I picked up a magazine and came back here to the hotel and read and watched TV for the rest of the evening."

Our local paper gave the story the full treatment as was fitting with such an important figure in the community. There was a full biography along with quotes from famous people about his book; there was a long statement from the police, a statement from me that included my theory of the time of death, the statements of Mrs. Hanrahan, Professor Ladlo and Dykes together with pictures of each, and finally an editorial gently chiding the police for inadequately safeguarding the dangerous site.

Professor Bowman was buried the day after Christmas. It was a small turnout. Johnny's son stood bareheaded, his hands clasped behind him, his handsome face impassive. He left immediately after the service.

The next day, Nicky Welt returned from Chicago. He had known Bowman for a long time and been friendly with him.

I told him all the circumstances of his death and the results of our investigation in detail. At the end, he pursed his lips and remarked. "It's very curious."

"What's curious?"

"Johnny must have been at least sixty—"

"Sixty-one, according to his son."

"Very well, sixty-one. A man who has lived that long has usually learned to avoid the more obvious dangers."

"So?"

"So it's curious that he'd get so close to the edge of an excavation that he'd tumble in."

"It happens all the time. And remember there was snow and the ground was slippery."

"Yes, I suppose so."

The college flag remained at half mast for a week, and then everyone returned from vacation, and it was as though Johnny Bowman had never been. It was a phenomenon that I had observed before.

Even Dykes, who had been closest to him, rarely mentioned him. As a matter of fact, he had a brand-new interest: the faculty chess tournament. He was on the Executive Committee of the club and was in charge. Since he was one of the best players, with an excellent chance of becoming champion, small wonder that he went about his task with enthusiasm.

Nicky and I had just finished lunching at the club when we came upon him tacking up the results of the draw on the bulletin board. Seeing Nicky, he said, "Hullo—we're matched in the first round."

"So we are," said Nicky. "I'm free at the moment if you'd care to play and get it over with."

"I've got all afternoon," said Dykes, "but Laura may call and I ought to be home to receive her call. She's still in Florida, you know." His face brightened. "Unless you'd care to come over to my place and play there. I've got a board and tournament chessmen. I'd like you to see my house," he added.

Nicky gave me a questioning glance and I shrugged my shoulders. "Very well, I'd like a bit of a walk."

"We go up High Street," Dykes said. "It's a bit of a climb."

"My office is in Lever Hall, young man," said Nicky with some asperity, "and I make it by way of High Street every day."

As we strode along, the wind whistled down the street and we had to lean forward against it. Dykes marched on his long legs and Nicky and I strove to keep up with him. A couple of times I thought Nicky would have liked to stop to catch his breath—I know I would have—but it was a point of pride with him not to show any weakness, and we continued without a stop until we reached the crest of the hill. There Dykes stopped.

"My place is over there. You can just see the roof from here."

"Why, it's not far at all," I said.

"About a hundred yards as the crow flies," he said. "But unfortunately it's a lot farther by foot."

Nicky nodded and then walked over to the other side of the road. "And this is where poor Bowman fell, eh?"

Since the accident, the police had put up a sturdy barrier of chain link fencing which made it impossible to approach to the edge.

"If they'd had a fence like that up, Bowman would have been alive today," Dykes remarked.

From there on it was downhill and the going was much easier. The street on which Dykes lived was a short private way with just his house and one other facing it that might have been its twin. They were both Victorian houses with numerous turrets and gables and tiny porches that served no really useful purpose.

Dykes stood back in obvious admiration. "What do you think of it? Of course it needs a lot of work, and I'll be busy with putty and paint for most of the summer, I guess, but I feel I've got something here to work on." He led us up the steps to the front door. He unlocked it, and stood back proudly. "Look at that—almost three inches thick. And that lock and the door handle—and this knocker. Solid brass all of it and heavy. I'll bet you couldn't replace this knocker alone for fifty dollars."

The door opened on a small vestibule, just beyond which was a large square reception hall, unfurnished except for a coat rack. Dykes snapped on a light and we could see a large room on either side, and like the reception hall, unfurnished.

From below came the sound of a dog barking and a moment later we heard him scratching on a door in the rear of the house, demanding to be let out.

Dykes smiled. "Good old Duke."

"Aren't you going to let him out?" I asked.

"He's better off down there," he said. Then in a tone of sharp command, "Down, Duke, down. Quiet." The barking and scratching stopped immediately and we heard him obediently trot down the stairs. Dykes listened to the dog's retreating footsteps and grinned smugly at the dog's training.

He led us to a broad staircase, and as we started upstairs said, "Take a look at that balustrade, will you. That's solid mahogany." He rapped it with his knuckles.

He led us into a room on the second floor that evidently served as the living room. This too was sparsely furnished with several armchairs, a coffee table and a rug, probably the furnishings of their former apartment but now quite lost in this new spaciousness. Over near the window, in an alcove, was a small round table with a chessboard and a box of chessmen. Two bridge chairs were drawn up to it, and Dykes left the room to return with a third.

Dykes drew white and won the first game in little more than twenty moves. As they turned the board around for the second game—the rules called for the best out of three games—Dykes said, "I guess that gambit was a little strange to you."

It was certainly strange to me. He had opened by advancing the king's rook pawn to the fourth. It was probably the worst move on the board and one which I could not recall having seen used except by the veriest beginner. It was as though he were deliberately handicapping himself to make up for the advantage of drawing white, and I thought he was showing a form of courtesy toward his older opponent who was also a guest in his house. Then it occurred to me that by throwing away his first move perhaps he wanted only to show how lightly he held Nicky. But as the game progressed, the initial move somehow became the focus for a strong attack on Nicky's king after he had castled. And then quite suddenly, the attack appeared to be a mere diversion and he captured the queen. Nicky had no choice but to resign.

He grunted in acknowledgment of defeat and put down his king. Nicky is not a good loser. They had not played more than half a dozen moves of the second game when we heard a bell ring somewhere toward the back of the house.

"Is that the call you were expecting?" I asked.

"No, that's the doorbell." He left the room and we could hear him shout down the stairwell, "Come on up."

He escorted into the room a young man of his own age with reddish-brown hair and a white freckled face with sharp knowing features. He was dressed in a leather windbreaker with a fur collar. A small foreign camera with a large protruding lens dangled from his neck by a leather strap. Dykes introduced him as his friend Bud Lesser.

Dykes did not offer to get him a chair and Lesser did not seem to expect one. He stood there, one hand resting on the back of Dykes' chair, his eyes flicking from the board to the faces of the players.

"Do you play, Mr. Lesser?" I asked out of politeness.

"Some."

"He beats me more often than I beat him," Dykes said. He made his move and then leaned back lazily and said, "How do you like my camera, Bud?"

His friend shrugged. "I don't know. Haven't had time to do a full roll yet. I'll know better when I develop what I've got in here."

Nicky in the throes of deciding on his next move glared at the two, and Dykes immediately turned his attention to the board. I, too, concentrated on the board. It seemed to me that Nicky had a slight advantage. He made his move and we all relaxed a little.

"I've got a Schlossmann antenna you can have if you're interested," Lesser volunteered.

"Oh yeah? When did you get it?"

"It's the one I got for myself, but I decided not to use it. My place is too low. I bought two and installed one for Arnold Sterling across the way. He tells me it works fine."

Dykes glanced at the board and negligently pushed a pawn. "I didn't know he had one. When did you put it up?"

"You can see it from here," said Lesser, nodding toward

the window. Dykes left the chess table and went to the window to look out. "He wanted it for Christmas, so the day before I came down at noon and by two o'clock I had it up."

Dykes returned to his seat. "If I had seen you, I would have given you a hand."

"I saw *you*," said Lesser.

"You couldn't have, I was away all day." Nicky made his move and he made his own immediately after. The game had reached a critical point and Nicky's brow was furrowed as he concentrated on the position. Dykes, too, was hunched forward as he studied the board.

As Nicky reached forward to move his piece, there was a flash of light and the simultaneous snick of a camera shutter. Nicky looked up indignant.

Lesser grinned. "Sorry, I just couldn't resist that shot—the afternoon sun slicing in through the slats of those venetian blinds on you, Bob, like you was dressed in prison stripes."

"Bud has a great eye for trick camera shots," Dykes offered by way of apology for his friend. He concentrated on the board for a long minute. Then smiling, he made his move and favored me with a wink. The advantage was clearly with him now. He was completely relaxed as he said to Lesser, "What are you asking for the antenna?"

"Five hundred."

Dykes whistled. "I couldn't manage it."

"I'll take three hundred and your camera."

Nicky moved and Dykes turned his attention once more to the board. He had a clear win and his next move seemed obvious, but he took a long time thinking about it. Finally he made it and turned once again to Lesser.

"Installed?" he asked. "I'd want it right above that dormer window in back."

"Fine with me. I'll put it any place you like."

"It's pretty high-up in one of the gables. Will you need any help?"

"No, I can put it up myself all right. I've got a magnesium ladder and it's no trouble."

"Okay, when we finish here I'll show you where I want it."

The game did not last much longer. Another half dozen moves and again Nicky put down his king in acknowledgment of defeat. We followed Dykes downstairs, and then because he seemed to expect it and because by now we were somewhat curious, we followed him to the yard in back of the house. Dykes pointed up at the roof. "There," he said. "Can you put it up right there?"

Lesser looked up. "Sure. I can rest my ladder right here in front of the cellar bulkhead."

"See that molding in the corner? Can you attach it to that?"

"Sure, no sweat. I'll use an angle bracket. Tomorrow be all right? Around noon?"

"Fine."

Lesser left and Dykes finished showing us around. "What do you think of it?" he asked eagerly. "Do you see what I mean when I say it's solid and built to last?"

Nicky pointed out the cellar bulkhead doors where Lesser proposed to set his ladder. "I notice you've had to do some modernizing," he remarked wryly. "Those don't look very solid."

Dykes grinned. "I guess there are some things you

can't have too solid. The original bulkhead doors weighed a ton and they were pretty far gone. I could have patched them, but as you know bulkhead doors don't just swing on a hinge—you've got to lift them. I was worried for Laura when she had to take her wash from the basement out to the yard. She couldn't manage those heavy doors so I installed these aluminum ones. These, a child can lift."

On the way back, I was tempted to tease Nicky about the quality of his chess. "You were not doing too badly in that second game," I said. "For a while I thought you might even pull out a win."

Absentmindedly he agreed. "He does play well, doesn't he? All slapdash and daring and full of surprises." Then he smiled and added, "But I was so absorbed in the conversation between Dykes and his friend that, frankly, I lost interest in the game."

Nicky always offers excuses for losing at chess.

The next day, Nicky and I had just finished lunch at the Faculty Club and were heading back to his office when Dykes joined us and said, "Say, if you fellows are going up High Street, I'll come along if you don't mind."

I am not at all sure that Nicky didn't mind—the defeat still rankled—but of course he couldn't very well refuse. As we walked along Dykes explained that Lesser was going to put up the new antenna and he felt he ought to give him a hand.

When we came to the top of the hill, Dykes pointed. "Why, there he is now." We followed the direction of his finger and to be sure could see in the distance a tiny figure on a ladder, working away at the edge of the roof. We watched for a moment and then started off. Dykes, who had stopped to tie his shoelace, hurried to catch up and we went on together to Nicky's office. We stood on the sidewalk talking. Then just as Nicky turned to leave, Dykes exclaimed, "Why here comes Duke." He squatted down on his haunches and called, "Here, boy." The dog increased his speed as he sighted his master and came bounding up, dancing around Dykes until his master ordered him sharply, "Down, Duke. Sit." Immediately the dog obeyed and sat motionless, a mound of iron-gray fur except for the ridiculous red flannel tongue which vibrated ecstatically. From deep in his throat came urgent whiny sounds.

"It's just as if he's trying to tell me something, isn't it?" Dykes remarked. "All right, boy, come on." He waved farewell to us and walked off down the road, the dog pacing sedately by his side.

"Smart dog," I remarked.

"Well trained," Nicky amended.

"Well, there's no doubt that the master is plenty smart," I said maliciously, attributing his curt reply to yesterday's defeat.

He did not deign to answer, but turned on his heel and mounted the stairs. I chuckled at the thought that I had reached him—it didn't happen often.

Nothing at my office demanded my attention and I was in no hurry to get back. So I strolled back by way of the campus where I bumped into Professor Zelsky, with whom I had been matched for the first round of the tournament. He was also free, so we returned to the Faculty Club and played our match which I won handily in two straight games. It gave me considerable satisfaction to know that

I had at least made the second round while Nicky had been eliminated in the first.

I played another half dozen games with Zelsky, losing when I gave him an advantage but invariably winning when we played even. He invited me to dinner at his house and it was quite late by the time I finally got home.

Dressing the next morning I turned on the news broadcast and heard that Lesser had been killed by a fall from a ladder while working on Professor Robert Dykes' house.

I had only met Lesser once, two days before, and had not found him particularly prepossessing; nevertheless it was something of a shock to realize he was now dead. What made it even worse was that apparently I had last seen him only minutes before his death.

I arrived at my office and to my surprise found Nicky waiting. He tapped an inside page of the morning newspaper and tossed it on my desk. "Have you seen this?"

A glance at the headline told me it was the story on Lesser. "I got it over the radio this morning," I said.

"I thought you might have more information."

I riffled through the papers on my desk. "Nothing here. But we can step around the corner to Police Headquarters and see what they've got." I was somewhat surprised he was interested, but knowing how I felt I assumed he felt the same way.

Captain Scalise was busy checking through the contents of a metal file on his desk when we came in. "This is luck," he said. "I was just planning to drop around to see you."

"Oh?"

"Yes sir. A man, name of Lesser—"

"That's why we're here," I said.

"Then you heard about it?"

"On the morning newscast. It didn't say much. Was there some reason you thought his death might interest me?"

"Well, there is and there isn't," said Scalise. "Seems this Lesser had a little shop where he repaired radios and TVs. He also did some film developing and printing. And he traded in cameras and sold supplies for ham operators. The story as I get it was that he was putting up some special kind of antenna for Professor Dykes. I guess you two must know him."

Nicky and I nodded.

"Well, along about half past one another professor from the college, name of Jan Ladlo, comes calling on Dykes. He rings the bell and there's no answer. So he goes around the back. According to him, Dykes frequently works around the back of the house and doesn't always hear the bell. At least that's what he says." He looked at us questioningly.

"Go on."

"Well, his story is that just as he rounded the corner of the house he heard a cry, and looking up, he saw the ladder falling. A moment later Lesser hit the ground. He rushed over, but immediately saw there was nothing to do. He ran out into the street and caught hold of Jeb Grogan, who is the patrolman on the beat. According to Grogan, Lesser was already dead, but of course he called in for an ambulance."

Scalise opened a desk drawer and took out a large manila envelope. He slid the contents onto the top of the desk. "This is what was found on him."

It was about what you would expect: a well-worn wallet

with eight dollars in bills, a pocket handkerchief, seventy-three cents in coin, and a leather key case. He poked in the still open drawer and this time drew out a camera with a leather case and strap. "And he was wearing this at the time. Kind of funny—I mean a man wearing a camera while working on a ladder."

"He was testing it. I gather he carried one pretty much all the time."

"Testing it to decide whether to buy it or not?"

"That's right."

"Then that checks. This fellow Dykes called up and asked if he could have it—claimed it was his and that you knew about it."

"Is that why you wanted to see me?"

"That was one of the reasons."

"What time did this happen—I mean Lesser falling?" asked Nicky.

Scalise flipped the pages of a notebook. "It was one fifty-two when Grogan saw the body. Figure that Lesser fell a couple of minutes earlier, maybe as much as five minutes because this Ladlo didn't spot Grogan right away."

I looked at Nicky. "That must have been within minutes after we saw him from High Street."

Nicky nodded grimly.

Scalise picked up the key case. "This kind of roused my curiosity," he said.

I opened it and found it contained three keys, one of which was obviously the key to his car. "What makes these so interesting?"

"Well, I know Lesser's shop," said Scalise. "It's a little two-by-four place and he lives in the back. I wouldn't give you a hundred dollars for everything in it. Now this key is the key to the shop, but this one is to a safe deposit box down at the bank. I know because I've got one. So I decided to take a look at the contents of that box. I also had the boys in the squad car look over his place. They brought this file in. It has some papers, but they're mostly bills and invoices and business correspondence. Nothing that helps us. There are also a bunch of pictures—"

"Pictures that Lesser snapped?" asked Nicky. "May I?"

"Sure." Scalise pushed the file over to him.

"Did the bank manager let you open Lesser's box?" I asked.

"Oh, I went to see Judge Quigley first of course. As a matter of fact, I know the manager and he would have let me look—unofficially, of course. He knows I'd play fair; if I found something, I'd leave it until I came back with a court order."

"That's all right then."

"These pictures are extremely interesting," said Nicky, who had been studying them all the while.

"Interesting how?" asked Scalise, fearful he had overlooked something.

"They're all the same kind of thing—what the art critics call *coup d'oeil*, the blink-of-an-eye type of picture, a flash of visual impression that is almost deceptive. There are action pictures here, for example, of a basketball game in which the players are like figures in a ballet; there's a picture of a full moon transfixed on the spire of a steeple like a ball on a Christmas tree; there is a picture of two people on a park bench that looks like a single body with two heads."

Scalise laughed. "Well, he took one other picture that isn't in that collection. It's like the blink of an eye all right.

In fact, it will make you blink. That's what I found in the safe deposit box. That's all that was there." He reached into his desk drawer and tossed over to me a small square print. It was of Professor Ladlo and his young wife. They were naked.

"A Peeping Tom," I exclaimed.

"Worse than that," said Scalise. "Turn it over."

On the back, in pencil, was a list of dates and beside each a sum of money.

"You'll notice that starting in May and going through to December, there is a hundred dollars a month that I'm guessing Ladlo paid to Lesser."

"Blackmail?"

"I would say so, sir."

"They've only been married a few weeks—"

"Oh, that's his wife, is it?"

"But the dates and figures would suggest that this happened sometime ago, months ago." I chuckled. "Sonofagun, I didn't think he had it in him."

Nicky cocked a quizzical eyebrow at me. "The initiative could have come from the lady, you know. She has a forceful personality."

"Nicky!"

"Obviously he was on a ladder when he took the shot," he continued, ignoring my outburst.

"How do you know?" asked Scalise.

"Because that took place in Ladlo's apartment. I've been there and I recognize the lamp on the table. Now Ladlo is on the third floor of that new apartment house on Dalton Street. Since there are only one- and two-story houses across the street he wouldn't have to draw the blinds. You can't see into his apartment from any of the houses across the way. But a man on a ladder putting up an antenna on the roof of one of those houses would be on the third-story level and could see straight in."

"I guess you're right," said Scalise. "That must have been the way it was done. In any case, you can see that I was justified in calling in Ladlo to make a statement."

"You showed him the snapshot?" I asked.

"No, I thought I ought to speak to you about it first, him being a professor at the college and all that. But knowing about the print, I thought it gave me the right to ask a lot of questions and get a full statement."

"What sort of questions?"

"The sort of questions you'd ask if you were investigating a crime," he answered sharply, "rather than what you'd need to just fill out an accident report. I asked him why he was calling on Dykes in the first place. You see, if he said he just happened to be in the neighborhood, he could have just happened to see Lesser on top of that ladder. A man on a ladder, Professor," he added with a smile, "can not only see a great distance, but he can also be seen."

"Your idea is that Ladlo might have spotted Lesser on the ladder, approached unnoticed, and upset the ladder?" Nicky asked.

"Why not?"

"It was a magnesium ladder and they're pretty easy to upset," Nicky admitted.

"That's right," Scalise said.

"And what reason *did* Ladlo give for being there?" I asked.

"He said he went to see Dykes about some manuscript he was working on. You remember this Professor Bowman who took a tumble a couple of weeks ago up at the excavation on High Street? He was writing a book with this Dykes, or Dykes was helping him. Now Bowman's son"—he glanced at his notes—"that'd be Charles Bowman, he's in the publishing business, and he's interested in getting that book for his own company. And as the old man's heir, I guess he's got a right to it, at least to that part of it that his father did. But according to Ladlo, he was afraid that if he came right out and asked for it, Dykes might balk—try to palm him off with a couple of chapters, claim that the rest was his, or that it was all that had been done. So he asked Ladlo to see Dykes so he could evaluate the manuscript."

"But why Ladlo? Did he know him?"

"He met him at Prex's party, of course," Nicky observed. "It would be the natural thing to do—to approach the senior man in the department."

"I gather too, the young feller hinted that he'd let him finish it, either with Dykes or alone," said Scalise.

"And did Bowman come to see him? He was here in town?" I asked.

"That's what Ladlo said."

"Did you check?"

"I called the hotel and he had been there all right but had already left by the time I called. Anyway, that was Ladlo's reason for going to see Dykes. And by the way, that's why he didn't phone first to make an appointment. I got the impression that Ladlo thought Dykes might not be too willing to surrender the manuscript. His idea was just to drop in on Dykes accidentally—as though he just happened to be in the neighborhood and then lead the talk around to the manuscript."

I glanced at Nicky. "What do you think?"

"I think the manuscript might be valuable enough to murder for," said Nicky quietly. "And I think there might be proof in that camera, Captain. I suggest you have the film in it processed right away."

"You think Lesser might have had a chance to snap a picture of Ladlo just before he fell, maybe even caught him in the act of tipping the ladder?" He looked at Nicky in frank admiration. He flipped the intercom switch on his desk and called in the uniformed officer who acted as his clerk. "Tom, take this down to Ned at the photo lab and tell him I want the roll in it developed and printed right away."

"But it wasn't Ladlo who wanted the manuscript," I protested, "at least not for himself. It was young Bowman—"

"We've got only Ladlo's word for that," said Scalise. "Besides, Ladlo had reason for killing Lesser because he was blackmailing him."

"He *had* been," Nicky corrected. "But that was over and done with. The figures show that. There's a line under the December payment and the amount is totaled. Back in May or earlier, when the picture was taken, it could have done a lot of damage. The lady was suing for divorce at the time. But now that they're married, Ladlo had nothing to fear from him."

Scalise was nettled. "Yeah, but Ladlo lost eight hundred dollars in this little game of Lesser's, and as far as I'm concerned that's good enough reason for Ladlo to give him the old heave-ho when he saw his chance."

Nicky looked at him in surprise. "Do you really think so, Captain? Eight hundred dollars is a nice tidy little sum, but to a man in Ladlo's position, hardly ruinous. Jan Ladlo is a mild, gentle, scholarly type, not what I would call vengeful. It's hard for me to imagine him killing someone in cold blood because he had been mulcted of eight hundred dollars. And would he have gone looking for a policeman? When he could have walked quietly away?" He shook his head. "I doubt if he even knew who his blackmailer was. I doubt if Lesser would have approached him directly. My guess is that the arrangements were made by telephone and the money was sent to a box number at the post office. When Lesser saw the announcement of the marriage a few weeks ago, he knew that the game was up. It wouldn't surprise me if he sent him the negative as a wedding gift. That would explain why it wasn't in the safe deposit box with the print." Suddenly he began to laugh. "Yes, I'm sure of it. It's in keeping with Lesser's rather peculiar sense of humor."

"What do you know about Lesser and his sense of humor?" I asked scornfully. "You saw him for a minute yesterday, a hundred yards away. And the day before, you saw him for about ten minutes, and he spoke maybe thirty words."

"The conversation was short," he admitted, "nevertheless it was quite remarkable."

"What was remarkable about it?"

"Do you remember how it went?"

I flatter myself that as a result of years of courtroom experience in the examination of witnesses, I have developed a pretty good memory. "Not word for word," I said, "but I remember the gist of it. Dykes asked Lesser how he liked the camera and he answered that he didn't know yet because he was still testing it. Then Lesser asked

Dykes if he wanted to buy some special antenna that he had. Dykes asked him when he got it and Lesser said it was one that he had bought for himself but had decided not to use because his place was too low; that he had put one up on the house across the street and that it worked fine. All right so far?"

"You're doing fine."

"Okay. Then Dykes asked him when he had put it up and Lesser said he had installed it in time for Christmas. And Dykes said he would have helped him if he had seen him working. And Lesser answered that he had seen *him*. So Dykes said he couldn't have because he had been away all day."

"And what did Lesser say to that?"

"He didn't say anything."

"That was what was remarkable about the conversation."

"I don't get it."

"Of course you don't." Nicky was scornful. "It's your courtroom training. In the courtroom, dialogue is carried on according to a rigid set of rules: a question is asked and the question is answered—finis. If you should repeat the question, the attorney on the other side or the judge would object that you had already asked your question and received an answer. Then there would be a discussion and finally the judge would rule that the witness did have to answer or did not. Then the witness would ask to have the question repeated—and on and on. But normal conversation doesn't work that way. It has a certain rhythm. When Dykes said that Lesser couldn't have seen him on the day in question because he was out of town, Lesser should have said something like, 'Well, I thought it was you,' or 'I could have sworn it was you,' or even, 'I guess I must have been mistaken.' But Lesser said nothing, and I lost all interest in the chess game because I was waiting for the other shoe to drop."

"But still I don't see—"

"—what connection it has with the present case? You've forgotten the day they were talking about. Lesser put up the antenna on the day before Christmas, the twenty-fourth. That was the day that Johnny Bowman fell to his death and that Dykes claimed to have been out of town all day."

I stared at him. "Are you suggesting that Bobby Dykes had something to do with Bowman's death?"

"He said he wasn't home when Bowman called because he was out of town. If he lied about seeing Bowman, it could be only because he had some knowledge of his death. And if he claimed he was in Norton all day, it can mean only that he wanted to furnish himself an alibi."

"But you don't know that he was home. Lesser said he saw him and Dykes denied it. And Lesser did not contradict him. And now Lesser is dead and we can't ask him."

"Ah, but he did contradict him. He dropped the other shoe all right, but I didn't know it at the time. Only when I saw this snapshot of Ladlo and his wife did I understand. He answered Dykes by snapping a picture of him and then explained that he couldn't resist the shot, what with the sun slanting through the venetian blinds like prison stripes. In effect, he was saying that he had proof of having seen him—that he had a picture of him. Dykes understood all right because it was then that he asked how much he wanted for the antenna. And if he had any doubt, it was dispelled when Lesser quoted him a price of five hundred dollars."

"You mean that five hundred was a blackmail payment? How do you know? What do you know about the price of an antenna?"

"I'll admit I don't know much about antennae? antennas?" He cocked his head to one side to listen to the sounds. Then he nodded. "Antennas—I think I prefer the English plural; the Latin can be reserved for the apparatus of insects."

"Nicky!"

"Oh yes, well I don't know much about antennas, but I do know something about five hundred dollars. I saw the antenna that Lesser installed. It was a simple affair. Unless it is made of some precious metal instead of the steel it appears to be made of, I would say that five hundred was at least three or four hundred too much."

"But why would Dykes want to kill Bowman, and how would he go about it?"

"As to why, obviously to get control of Bowman's manuscript. It's expected to make a lot of money—"

"You mean he'll publish it as his own work?"

"Oh, hardly. He couldn't, and it would do him little good if he did since Bowman's name on the cover is what will sell it. But as matters stand now, no one knows how much of it has actually been done. He can easily claim that no more than half is finished. He will complete it and and thus become a co-author rather than a mere research assistant. His name will be on the cover with Bowman's. He will receive half the royalties. And the boost to his academic prestige will be enormous."

"I'll grant you that."

"As to how he did it," Nicky went on, "that presents no difficulties. He and Bowman were on High Street—perhaps on their way to meet young Bowman. At the top of the hill they stopped to rest and Dykes could have called Johnny over to look at the excavation. And when Bowman leaned over the edge . . ." He shrugged his shoulders.

"You mean he thought of it just like that, on the spur of the moment?" asked Scalise.

"Oh, he's a quick thinker, is our Professor Dykes. You've only to play chess with him to realize that. One glance at the board and he makes his move. But I'm inclined to believe that he had been thinking of this for some time. I fancy his wife sensed something—I find it suggestive that she went to visit her folks without him and still has not returned. One thing I'm sure of: Bowman never would have asked him to remain and work on the book while his wife went on vacation alone. Gentleman Johnny was a gentleman." He cocked a speculative eye on the ceiling. "I wonder what Dykes would have managed if young Bowman hadn't come—"

"Young Bowman? What did he have to do with it?" asked Scalise quickly.

"His coming forced Dykes' hand, of course. Once they went over the manuscript with Johnny's son, Dykes would have been estopped from claiming any major share in its authorship."

"Well, it's an interesting case you've made out, Professor," said Scalise grudgingly, "but I don't see that it does us much good. You'd never get a jury to convict on that kind of evidence. Dykes has only to deny everything, and with Lesser dead, there's no way of proving it."

"You're forgetting the picture Lesser took," said Nicky.

As if on cue, there was a knock on the door. "Got the pictures for you, Captain," the clerk said.

The film had rolled up into a tight cylinder from the drying process, and we crowded around Scalise as he weighted one end down with a ruler and unrolled it slowly, studying each frame as he did so. Not till the end of the strip did Nicky point triumphantly and exclaim, "There it is."

The Captain and I stared at the frame and then looked at each other, unbelieving. It was indeed a picture of two men—but so foreshortened that at first sight they looked more like short cylindrical stumps surmounted by round buttons which were their heads.

I began to laugh, quite uncontrollably, and Scalise joined me.

"And what do you find so amusing?" Nicky asked icily.

I pointed at the picture. "He bluffed him. The scoundrel bluffed him. There's nothing there that can be used as evidence. There's no way of proving that those are pictures of Dykes and Bowman. It could be any two people."

"Maybe we can bluff Dykes, too," Scalise suggested hopefully. "We don't have to show him the picture—just tell him we've got it and encourage him to confess."

"There is no need to bluff Dykes," said Nicky coldly. "The picture is valid evidence. Why do you suppose Lesser took it in the first place? Certainly not because he wanted a snapshot of his friend. That he could have taken any time. He didn't have to wait until he was clinging to a ladder thirty feet or more above ground. No, he looked down and saw two men leaning forward against the wind with only the tops of their heads showing, so that at first glance they looked like a couple of toadstools. And that was the kind of subject he enjoyed shooting—the *coup d'oeil.* It was only when he thought about it afterwards that it occurred to him that the picture would show one figure with a derby hat framed against the astrakhan coat collar and that had to be Bowman, and the other showed a white streak bisecting his black head of hair, and that could be none other than Dykes. And what is more, the snow on the ground showed that it was taken the day before Christmas—our first snowfall of the winter."

Scalise nodded slowly. He looked at me and said, "It adds up."

"All right," I said, "what do we do now?"

Nicky rose. He favored us with his frosty little smile, a pursing of the lips as though he had bit into a sour lemon. "I suggest that the good Captain might call Professor Dykes and tell him to come down to Police Headquarters to claim his camera."

It was not until we were back in my office that the thought occurred to me. "Nicky," I exclaimed, "there's something terribly wrong about our line of reasoning. We started out to inquire into Lesser's death. And then we got sidetracked into thinking about Johnny Bowman. But what about Lesser? Was his death an accident, one of those rare coincidences that occasionally do happen? Or was it murder? And if it was murder, it couldn't have been Dykes, because he was with us at the time. And if it wasn't Dykes, then it must have been someone else. And if it was someone else, then our reasoning on Dykes is wrong."

"Oh, Lesser was murdered all right, and it was Dykes who did it. I know how it was done, but I can't prove it, not that it makes any difference, since the penalty for two deaths is no greater than for one. It was indicated in that same remarkable conversation."

At my look of complete confusion, he adopted the tone he uses to address one of his slower students. "You remember after the price of the antenna was settled, Dykes asked if the fee included installation. And when Lesser agreed—"

"Dykes said he wanted it right above the dormer in back," I said testily. "I remember that."

Nicky chuckled. "It was like a chess game between those two, a chess game between two masters. You know, chess players of our caliber," he went on, "we're only too happy when we don't make any mistakes and don't fall into the more obvious traps. Theoretically, since everything is visible on the board, one ought to be able to counter every attack, however devious. But players like us, we can't help concentrating on what appears to be the main line of attack. We see the whole board, to be sure, but we concentrate only on the portion that appears to be threatened. But players of the caliber of Dykes and Lesser, they approach the game in a different spirit. The correct response to the position on the board is automatic with them. They play the man, concentrating on his psychological weaknesses.

"Oh, they were a precious pair of rascals. Lesser opened with a brilliant gambit. He not only made his blackmail proposition, but made it publicly under the very nose of the County Attorney."

"I suppose that's what you meant by his peculiar sense of humor."

"Precisely. Naturally he was elated—at his success, at his bravado, at his panache. When Dykes asked if the price of the antenna included installation, he interpreted it as an attempt to salvage something, however small, out of a bad bargain, like a chess player who tries to take a pawn or two when he finds he's going to lose his queen. He could afford to be generous, so he agreed. But Dykes had something else in mind. Oh, it was a magnificent counter! You remember how when I played with him, his attack on my king turned out to be a diversion so that he could capture my queen, like a stage magician who focuses your attention on one hand while he does something else with the other.

"He worked the same trick on Lesser. To locate the antenna above that particular dormer called for setting the foot of the ladder right in front of the bulkhead doors. And when we got out into the yard, he focused Lesser's attention on the roof and the top of the ladder, but it was the *foot* of the ladder and positioning it right in front of the bulkhead doors that really concerned him. And those doors, you will recall, were so light that a child could lift them."

"You mean that if anyone were to raise the bulkhead door it would upset the ladder?"

Nicky's little eyes were shining as he nodded.

"But dammit, that would mean that someone would have to be in the cellar. And it couldn't be Dykes because he was with us at the time."

"Naturally. He saw to that. We were his alibi."

I snapped my fingers. "His wife. She's been hiding out in the cellar all along and . . ." My voice trailed off at his look of derisive scorn. "I guess not. But," I protested, "Dykes didn't know he was going to have to kill Lesser until a couple of days ago."

"Precisely. Nevertheless there was a resident in the cellar, bigger and stronger than any child. A big brute of a dog. Dykes arranged to be with us as we walked up High Street. At the top of the hill, we stopped, and Dykes saw that Lesser was on the ladder. We walked on, but Dykes stopped to tie his shoe, and—"

"And what?"

"And blew his damn whistle."